BITTERSWEET KISSES

"You look beautiful tonight," he whispered.

"You needn't pay me empty compliments, Sir Neville."

"Empty? I don't know if you are being dishonest with yourself or begging for more, my dear."

Yes, this is merely a flirtation, thought Annabelle. She tried to think of some witty rejoinder, but a cloud had covered her heart, and she remained silent.

"Have I said something to upset you? You look unhappy all of a sudden," said Neville, his long fingers tilting her face up to meet his. Annabelle didn't resist, and his lips touched hers. His arms slipped around her, gently pulling her petite frame against him.

This, thought Annabelle, is not a dream; it is nothing like, and she responded in a manner long since forgotten. Her arms circled his neck, and she pressed her body along the entire length of his.

"Annabelle," he breathed, clinging to her, his lips resting against her hair as rational thought slowly returned.

Releasing her enough to look down, he lifted her chin again. Her eyes ~~~~ ~~~~ly, and he saw a thin tric~~~~ ~~~~ng slowly down her chee~~~~

"Wha~~~~ ~~~~ing to find her overcom~~~~

She sh~~~~ ~~~~g to her mouth to stifle a ~~sob~~. The expression of pain in her eyes was evident even in the darkened garden, and Neville stepped back in surprise. Annabelle fled.

WATCH FOR THESE REGENCY ROMANCES

THE FIRST WALTZ

Donna Bell

Zebra Books
Kensington Publishing Corp.

http://www.zebrabooks.com

ZEBRA BOOKS are published by

Kensington Publishing Corp.
850 Third Avenue
New York, NY 10022

First Printing: March, 1998
10 9 8 7 6 5 4 3 2 1

Printed in the United States of America

This book is dedicated to my colleagues and my students at Northwest High School in Justin, Texas.

Chapter One

"Not a word, young lady, not a word!"

"But, Mother!" began the fiery-haired beauty, hurrying after her angry parent.

"*Shh!*" hissed Lady Annabelle Fairfax, stopping suddenly on the top step. "Not until we are home! Where is Charlotte?"

"Here, my lady," squeaked this tall young lady.

With a flick of her hand, Lady Annabelle shooed her two charges into the waiting carriage. When her daughter would have spoken, she was quelled by one terrifying brow.

Twenty minutes later, the carriage came to a stop, and a footman threw open the door. Lady Annabelle descended and made her way through the elegant London town house without a backward glance. She knew the two girls would follow her all the way up to her sitting room. She also knew she was in for the usual tug of war with Phoebe, her headstrong daughter.

The door snapped closed, and Lady Annabelle sent

her maid away with a nod. Pulling off her evening gloves, she sat down in the most comfortable chair, smoothing her gown with maddening calm before looking up at the two beauties before her.

With a toss of her mop of unruly red curls, Phoebe sat down on the sofa. Her raven-haired friend Charlotte sat down also, but without the theatrical huff of indignation.

"Mother . . ." began Phoebe.

"My lady . . ." essayed Charlotte.

"No, this time you will listen while I speak. I don't want to hear a word from either of you until you have been made sensible of the gravity of your behavior this evening. I know this was your first ball, but did not Lady Margaret," she said with a speaking glance at Phoebe, and to Charlotte, "your mother, warn you expressly not to take to the floor when a waltz was being played?"

"Yes, Mother," and "Yes, Lady Annabelle," murmured the girls.

"Then what sort of mischief were you planning when you stepped to the floor? And do not tell me you didn't know it was a waltz! That is all the two of you talk about whenever a ball is mentioned!"

"We weren't going to dance the waltz," said Phoebe, lifting her head and facing her mother's ire head-on.

"Then why step onto the dance floor? Surely you don't mean to gammon me that Lord West and Mr. Good were forcing this folly on you!" As the girls shook their heads, Lady Annabelle continued. "Good. At least you have the courage to admit the fault was all yours."

"Mama, if you'll just listen for a moment, I'll explain what really happened." Phoebe Fairfax paused to be certain her mother had finished with her diatribe before she continued. Her lovely face, so very much like her mother's, tried to wear a humble expression, but it did not sit well. Trying to keep the defiance out of her voice, Phoebe said, "West did ask me to dance the waltz with him, but I told him I had not yet received permission from the holy patronesses ..."

"Phoebe!" said Lady Annabelle severely, managing to keep her amusement well hidden.

"Very well, the patronesses of holy Almack's. He was disappointed, as was Goodie, Charlotte's partner, so we decided to form a quadrille and dance that while the waltz was being played. Really, Mother, we are not so cork-brained as to risk acceptance into that hallowed hall by displeasing Lady Cowper or Lady Jersey, both of whom were in attendance. Actually, we thought we might begin a new trend, as it were, for the unblessed waltzless ladies."

Lady Annabelle schooled her features to severity, but it took a great deal of effort. Finally, she managed, "That's as it may be, but you must remember, Phoebe, and you too, Charlotte, the Ton deals in appearances, and your actions *appeared* to be defiant. It simply isn't done—especially by young ladies making their debuts into Society. There will not be a single gentleman willing to stand up with you for any dance should you disgrace yourselves. Now, I shan't say anything to your mother, Charlotte, but you must both remember to behave circumspectly in the future."

"Yes, Lady Annabelle. Thank you."

Charlotte hurried from the room, but Phoebe remained standing beside the sofa, looking off into space, her rosebud lips pursed most appealingly.

"Did you have something else to say, Phoebe?" asked her parent, her green eyes capturing her daughter's gaze and holding it.

"Yes, Mother. I understand you are only advising me on the Ton's mores, but I want you to know I think it is all poppycock. Not dance the waltz? Why, I've been dancing the waltz at home for over a year!"

"True, but that is in the provinces, and your partners were either myself or our ten-year-old stable boy. This is London."

Phoebe laughed. "Yes, it is difficult to understand the supposed 'dangers' of the waltz when one's partner is one's mother. But I think it is still poppycock."

"Phoebe, when you are married, you'll have more license to do as you please. Until then, you must be patient. Marriage will change everything."

"Patient," murmured Phoebe with another toss of her fiery curls. "And if this hypothetical husband forbids me do as I please? What then?"

Lady Annabelle laughed gently and stood up to give her daughter a hug. "Then, you will not care, for you will want to do as your beloved husband advises."

"I hope you are right, Mother, but then, you can hardly know. You've had only yourself to answer to for over eighteen years." With this, Phoebe kissed her mother's cheek and, with a wicked grin, waltzed gracefully out of the room.

Lady Annabelle Fairfax strolled to the mirror and inquired, "How will the two of us ever survive this Season?"

She smoothed the dark green silk of her evening gown, gazing at her image in the glass, but not really taking in the deep auburn curls or the fine green eyes, set in a face whose skin was still like porcelain.

Time had been very kind to Lady Annabelle Fairfax. Or perhaps, as the gallant old squire back home often remarked, Lady Annabelle's innate kindness and dutiful behavior held back the ravages of time. Indeed, at six and thirty, she was counted as beautiful now as she had been as a bride. Everyone in the parish agreed—time had only sharpened her beauty; her candid green eyes and dewy complexion still turned the heads of men and women. Her figure, having borne one daughter, was as trim as ever; perhaps the bosom was more generous, but that could hardly be counted a fault.

And finally, Lady Annabelle was getting a chance to shine, much to the delight of her friends back in Berkshire. The fact that this, her first journey to London, was for the occasion of bringing out her beautiful, willful daughter, was a shame, but everyone—except Lady Annabelle herself—fully expected her to capture the heart of some good, gallant gentleman.

Romance, however, was the last thing on Lady Annabelle's mind as she rang the bell for her maid.

"Mother! Not some musty old museum! Charlotte and I will simply die of ennui! We would much prefer going to the Pantheon Bazaar or Astley's Circus, wouldn't we, Charlotte?"

"Oh, Phoebe, I . . ." began the raven-haired Charlotte.

"Now, Phoebe, it is most unkind of you to put dear Charlotte in such an awkward position. We are going to see the paintings at the Royal Academy, and that's all there is to it! You, who were always railing against the dullness of education for young ladies, must surely see the benefits of being exposed to renowned works of art, even though the Academy is limited to male artists." Remembering her audience and tailoring her argument to one that might influence them, Annabelle said, "Besides, it's a topic you should be able to discuss intelligently with any young man you happen to meet. And I've already arranged it with Charlotte's mother."

Phoebe Fairfax rose up on the fainting couch and

swung her feet to the floor, a thoughtful expression replacing the former sullen frown.

"Very well, Mother, just give us half an hour to dress. We'll meet you downstairs." With a bright smile, she blew her mother a kiss and took her friend's hand, practically dragging her from the room.

Annabelle shook off the feeling of foreboding her daughter's cheerful acquiesce had engendered in her breast. She changed into a stylish carriage dress in a pale yellow wool crepe and settled a modish bonnet on her curls, tying the matching ribbons at a jaunty angle.

I will *not*, she promised herself, allow Phoebe to ruin this, my first visit to the wonderful exhibits at the Royal Academy. Finally, she thought, tripping down the steps, I will be able to see the masters' works.

A short time later, Annabelle heaved a sigh of admiration as she gazed raptly at the first painting they encountered.

Remembering the girls at her side, Annabelle said, "Now this landscape is by Mr. Turner. You see how subtle the reflection in the water is? Oh, how I wish I could—"

"Very nice," said her daughter Phoebe. "Mother, would it be all right if Charlotte and I wandered about on our own? As long as we don't venture too far away, that is."

"I suppose so. I realize you don't wish to study each work in as great a detail as I do. And I know I can count on you both to conduct yourselves with the greatest decorum." Lady Annabelle's tone left no doubt that she had no such confidence, and that she would be keeping an eye out for them.

"Mother! We're not schoolgirls anymore!"

"Really, Lady Annabelle . . ," said Charlotte.

"Very well, run along. Otherwise, you will only ruin

my visit. But Mary goes with you." The little maid
sketched a curtsey.

Phoebe gave her mother a quick buss on the cheek
before strolling away, both girls looking raptly, if quickly,
at the masterpieces surrounding them. Annabelle soon
lost all track of time as she took out her sketchbook
and tried to capture the general theme of several works.

In the next gallery, Sir Neville Colston sat on a bench
in front of a portrait of George III by Gainsborough,
his box of charcoals beside him as he shaded his drawing, trying to capture that same depth in his own sketch.
Finally, he sat back and closed his eyes.

This, he thought, is what it means to be civilized. All
that time fighting old Boney had made him appreciate
being English, being in civilized London, where one
could take time to appreciate art, music, and even conversation with a few, select friends.

His concentration was broken by the whisper of feminine voices. He remained very still, hoping the intruders
would pass without stopping to socialize. He preferred
to keep his conversation and art separate; recollections
of his last two visits when Lady Rand-Smythe had mysteri-
ously appeared made him cautious.

But the voices didn't pass him by, and with a start,
he realized they were on the other side of the immense
pillar at his back. Their giggles completely spoiled his
concentration. He stole a peek around the column and
his gray eyes widened in surprise as they removed their
cloaks.

The two young ladies, one red-haired and the other
dark, were dressed in the most rakish costumes he had
ever seen. He wondered briefly if they were lightskirts,
but their accents were too refined. Intrigued, he set
aside his sketch pad and listened unashamedly. A bit

of entertainment, he thought, rather like going to the theater.

"Lud," whispered their maid, looking around hastily.

"*Shh*, Mary, and go sit down over there on that bench. There's no need for you to be following us like a shadow."

"But, miss—"

"Don't worry. I'll tell my mother it was my idea. Besides, she knows that already. Remember Tunbridge Wells?"

Neville heard the little maid's footsteps retreat.

"Charlotte, you look so elegant."

"Uh, so do you, Phoebe," said the other voice.

"Well, I suppose the bodice is cut a little too low," replied the first young lady.

That one, that Phoebe, thought Neville, must be the one who looked like she should be some man's ladybird. What was her mother about letting the child go out dressed like that?

"But it was so dull when Madam Dufort finished it. I really thought it would be better without that lace inset, didn't you? It's no worse than Caro Lamb wears."

Ah, thought Sir Neville cynically, now there's a fashion leader to ape.

"I suppose not," the other one said doubtfully.

Someone ought to lock them up and throw away the key, thought Neville. They were obviously escaped schoolroom misses. They would be in for it when they were discovered going about London dressed as they were. But Sir Neville was in for more of a shock.

"I didn't realize it was quite so low. I shall simply have to breathe deeply to fill it up," Phoebe added.

"I'm not so certain this was wise," said her companion Charlotte. "What if one of the patronesses were . . ."

So, thought Sir Neville, they were young ladies, and well-placed ones at that.

"As if they come to this fusty old place," sneered Phoebe. "As a matter of fact, there doesn't seem to be anyone here, at least no one of importance. We should have warned Goodie and West we were going to be here in our finery, then we could have had a jolly time— even here. But I suppose if we want to find adventure, we'll have to look other places."

"Phoebe, I don't know. Why don't we put our cloaks back on?"

Now there is the voice of reason, thought Sir Neville.

"Nonsense! In for a penny, in for a pound. Besides, you look absolutely magnificent in that royal blue, much better than in sprig muslin. Now, let's pretend to be engrossed in some picture while we make our plans."

Plans, thought Neville, sitting up and taking notice. Now we're getting to the farce! But what followed contrived to shock the former major who had bravely confronted the French both in the Peninsula and at Waterloo. He had always suspected the female of the species was the better strategist, but these girls were bolder than any French Guard. He peeked around the corner and smiled when he noticed they were pretending to be enthralled by the magnificent portrait of a soldier mounted on a white steed, his sword drawn while the battle raged around him. How appropriate.

"So, where do we find this adventure?" asked the one he had identified as Phoebe.

"I'm not sure 'adventure' is the right word, but I've always wanted to go to Parliament," whispered Charlotte. "Only I think that's been done before."

"Well, then that should be our first objective, since we know it can be achieved. Something easy to get our feet wet, as it were. And then, what about that horse place?'' asked Phoebe.

Neville could hear the distaste in Charlotte's voice. "You know how I loathe horses, Phoebe. But I don't suppose an hour at Tattersall's would kill me."

"Good! Now, that takes care of the horses. What else do gentlemen do? I vowed to leave no stone unturned when I bet Tony Gilbreath back home that I would do everything he did when he came to London and more!" said Phoebe.

Neville turned on the bench, and a piece of charcoal hit the marble floor.

"What was that?" said the two girls.

They were silent for a moment before Phoebe continued.

"So what else do the gentlemen do that we're not supposed to do?" she asked.

"I have always wanted to learn how to fence. Do you suppose we might hire a fencing master? I believe I could be very good at a parry and thrust," said the redhead.

A wicked smile formed on Sir Neville's lip. The girl is both innocent and bold. Too bad she is a lady, he concluded. Still, these girls might make for an interesting Season.

"I don't know about fencing, but there is Gentleman Jackson's boxing salon," said the dark-haired girl.

But the other said hastily, "Pugilists? No, I thank you, but that is out of the question, even for us! What else?"

Neville breathed a sigh of relief, running a hand through his dark hair and shaking his head. It just kept getting worse and worse! Really, he would need to discover their parents and . . . tattle? The thought left a bitter taste in his mouth.

"My father spends a great deal of time at his club.

It's full of stuffy politicians, but the really fashionable go to White's. I've always wanted to go, too. You know, to find out what the attraction is. Wouldn't it be a lark to wager a fortune on the turn of a card!''

White's! marveled Neville. These girls were highly placed indeed, although their social position would be ruined if they carried through with their madcap schemes.

"White's?" said the one called Phoebe. "I'm afraid we might be recognized there. Maybe we could go some place less well attended."

"I have heard rumors of some newer clubs in Pall Mall."

"Good! Pall Mall, it is!" said Phoebe.

Charcoal and sketchbook flying, Neville jumped to his feet and stepped around the huge pillar, bearing down on the pair with a terrible frown. They had gone too far!

"Good God, young woman! Have you no modesty! Of all the featherbrained schemes! Your fathers should take a horse-whip to you! The next thing I hear, you'll be gambling at the Devil's Den like common lightskirts!"

"Sir! What is the meaning of this?" exclaimed Lady Fairfax, hurrying across the marble floor, her skirts raised just enough to afford Sir Neville a view of kid slippers and neat ankles.

Phoebe groaned and grumbled, "It needed only this."

"We can explain—" croaked Charlotte.

"Silence," snapped Lady Annabelle and Sir Neville at the same time before glaring at each other again.

"Are you in charge of these ..." Here, Sir Neville raked the girls' audacious gowns with his cold silver gaze. "... young women?" he finished.

Phoebe's eyes flew to her mother's face; surely the

wrath of God was about to be called down on this hand-some—if older—gentleman. She had seen men crumble beneath her mother's cold stare.

But Lady Annabelle, for the first time in her life, was robbed of her usually breathtaking power of speech. She couldn't even muster up the ability to analyze the cause—but the contemptuous glare of the handsome gentleman in front of her somehow entered into this temporary incapacity for attack. His dark hair was silvering at the temples, his clothes were of the first stare, and his cold gray eyes were as forbidding as a tomb.

"I am in charge of these young ladies," Lady Annabelle managed finally.

His tone as disdainful as a royal prince, Sir Neville Colston said, "Then, my good woman, I suggest you keep them locked in the schoolroom until you make certain they are gowned as befits young ladies, and until someone more fitting has instructed them on how ladies conduct themselves in the polite world."

"I beg your pardon!" snapped Lady Annabelle, her breast now heaving with indignation.

But before she could continue, Sir Neville cut her off. "And so you should, madam, else I will be forced to inform your employer of your incompetence!"

With a curt nod, he retrieved his sketchbook and charcoals and stalked away, cursing under his breath at the waste of the afternoon light and the folly of allowing young females to appear anywhere in public.

By the time Lady Annabelle had regained the power of speech, the abigail had thrown the modest cloaks around Phoebe and Charlotte, and they hurriedly fastened them. When Annabelle turned around, her left eyebrow was climbing toward the errant auburn curl that had escaped her modish bonnet.

"How dare you cause such an uproar!" she whispered through clenched teeth.

"But, Mother, we were only looking at the pictures and talking."

"Hmph! And don't bother to finish with those buttons, young lady. I got quite an eyeful when I arrived on the scene. Those gowns are going in the fire."

"But, Mama, some poor, needy person—"

"Hmph! Come along! We're going home!"

Phoebe swallowed hard, her large green eyes now glistening with tears. "Home to . . . ?"

"To Charlotte's," snapped Lady Annabelle, turning on her heel and marching away. Exchanging unrepentant grins, the girls followed.

The girls remained silent all the way home, but Lady Annabelle mumbled under her breath, shaking her head from time to time, sending her still-auburn curls bouncing.

When they entered the door, Lady Margaret Sweet was hurrying to meet them, her bountiful frame shimmying in its stays as if trying to break free.

"Oh, my dear Annabelle! The most wonderful thing happened while you were out! Lady Jersey called and left vouchers for both our girls!"

"For Almack's!" exclaimed the two girls simultaneously.

"How fortuitous," murmured Lady Annabelle. "First, I think they should go upstairs and change. Don't you agree, girls?"

"Yes, Mother," said Phoebe humbly.

"Oh, yes, my lady," echoed Charlotte.

When they returned, they were dressed in virginal white, their hair held demurely away from their faces with single strands of ribbon. Annabelle found it difficult to keep a straight face. Her daughter was such a schemer!

Her old friend Margaret was in the middle of her tale of triumph about the visit from Almack's exalted patroness, and Annabelle didn't wish to interrupt. The girls sat on the windowseat and put their heads together. Annabelle could just overhear their conversation while lending half an ear to Margaret's story.

Phoebe whispered, "Vouchers for Almack's!"

"They couldn't have come at a better time!" exclaimed Charlotte. "Now they'll never pack us up and send us away to Great Aunt Hildegard!"

"Charlotte, is there truly a Great Aunt Hildegard? You have been talking about being exiled to her estate in the wilds of Yorkshire since we met at school, but I have never really been sure you were serious."

Charlotte was shaking her head and rolling her eyes. "Oh, yes, and I have even received a letter from her! Last November when I turned eighteen, she wrote to tell me she would be happy to help find me a husband! Can you imagine what kind of man an eighty-year-old spinster rusticating in the countryside might think a suitable husband!"

"Anyone still breathing, I would guess!" whooped Phoebe, forgetting where she was in her merriment.

"Yes, and with a dozen motherless children!" added Charlotte, covering her mouth with her hands to stifle her laughter.

"A roof of sod!" added Phoebe.

"A floor of sand!"

"What is the meaning of this!"

Both girls sat up immediately, their eyes coming to rest on the massive, heaving bosom of Charlotte's indignant mother. They had laughed over that before, too, but their moods were decidedly subdued by her sudden question.

"I asked you a question, Charlotte Annabelle Christine Sweet!" demanded her mother, sailing closer to the windowseat.

Lady Annabelle bit the inside of her cheek to contain her laughter and kept her eyes away from her daughter's gaze. Lady Margaret Sweet had no idea of the spectacle she created, like a frigate under full sail, or perhaps a better analogy was one of those modern ships which belched steam. Lady Annabelle shook herself mentally; even if her rapscallion of a daughter didn't, she knew the importance of Margaret's maternal message and schooled her own features to one of cool disapproval.

"How could you appear in public wearing those . . . gowns!" Lady Sweet filled the words with such disgust, both girls dropped their eyes and studied the tops of their shoes.

"We're sorry, Mama," whispered Charlotte.

Lady Margaret sighed and shook her head. The wind has gone out of her sails, thought Annabelle.

"My dear child, I have tried to tell you, time and again, that you must be satisfied with your muslin gowns for the time being. They are suitable to your station. Your day will come when you may wear silks and satins." She smoothed her rich purple gown complacently. "In the meantime, be satisfied. You both look so charming in your sprig muslins. Don't they, dear Annabelle?"

"Indeed, one could almost believe they had been schooled to behave like young ladies. However, such a deception will not pass muster under the eagle scrutiny of the Ton."

Phoebe chuckled.

"Was there something you wished to say, young lady?" asked her mother, that arched brow shooting upward.

"No, ma'am," said Phoebe quietly.

Annabelle took full responsibility for Phoebe's tendency to treat such a lofty subject as fashion with inappropriate levity. Hadn't she raised her daughter to think for herself? But now was not the time to encourage such a trait.

"Then there will be no more outlandish costumes?"

"No, Mother," echoed both girls.

"Perhaps there will be an opportunity for you to show off your elegant sartorial splendor during the Season," said Lady Sweet. "I happen to know we will be invited to Lady Grosbeck's masqued gala."

"A masquerade!" breathed all her listeners—two with amazed delight and one with ill-concealed dismay.

At their barrage of questions, Lady Sweet waved her hands and smiled benignly. "All in good time, all in good time. Now, you girls must rest before our card party tonight. Lady Annabelle and I have a few calls to make."

The two young women fell instantly into a discussion of costumes for the promised masqued ball.

At the door, however, Lady Sweet turned and said sternly, "Just remember, Charlotte, only obedient girls will be allowed to attend the masquerade. Other girls will be sent to stay with Great Aunt Hildegard!"

The door closed, but Annabelle could still hear the girls' shouts of laughter, and she smiled.

Was she ever so young and silly? Perhaps if she had ever had a Season, she mused. But being married at seventeen to a man twice her age, she had easily slipped into the role of matron and soon after—mother. Her husband had succumbed to a fever after only six months of marriage, and Annabelle, five months pregnant, had been obliged to become estate manager as well.

No, she concluded with something approaching a sigh, she had never been so young and silly.

Coming to attention as Sir Neville entered his library, Maltby managed to refrain from saluting as he said, "Major, sir, you're back early today."

Neville waved the older man back into his chair behind the huge oak desk as he strode to the sideboard and poured a generous measure of Madiera. He cocked his head to one side in question, but Maltby shook his head and sat down again.

"Demmed females," grumbled Neville.

"Surely you didn't run into Lady Rand-Smythe at the museum again?"

"Hah! No, this time it was two young chits!" Neville sat down in the chair opposite his desk and took a quick gulp of the fiery liquid.

"Chits? Didn't know you could be so disturbed by the schoolroom set. Am I to wish you happy?" asked his former batman with glee.

Maltby had been a veteran campaigner before becoming Sir Neville's batman. His practical lessons had kept Neville both sane and alive when he first arrived in Spain. Their relationship, now that they had left the army, was comfortable, less employer and employee than that of old, familiar comrades.

So Sir Neville took no offense, only frowning and saying distractedly, "Lud, no. I've no designs in that area. Though there was the usual chaperon, you know."

"A dragon of a woman," said Maltby knowingly.

"No, no, not this one. You know, Maltby, I don't know when I've seen such green eyes. Sort of like the sky . . . only green of course. Or perhaps a field of freshly sickled . . . It's rather too difficult to describe. Think I'll just go find my paints," added Neville, pulling his long, lean form out of the chair with lazy grace.

Maltby's jaw, which had fallen open, snapped closed, and his bushy gray brows knit together. With a low rumble of laughter, he observed quietly to the empty room, "Not wishing you happy just yet, but it won't be long, not by my count."

"I heard that," called Sir Neville.

Neville made his way to the uppermost room of the house. Opening the door, he entered and stood on the threshold for a moment, surveying the room without really seeing it. He ambled to the window and opened it wide, allowing the late afternoon breeze to chase away the stale air. Below lay the gardens, and beyond the neatly ordered walks and plants, he could see into the small stableyard where his tiger was currying his gray mare.

He turned and sifted through a disorganized box of paints. Not finding what he was searching for, he pitched it back onto the table and picked up another.

"Kelly green," he said smearing a dab onto his finger. With a grunt, he added a speck of white.

Sitting down on a wooden stool, he took a pencil and began a rough sketch, shaking his head now and then.

Satisfied, he began adding the oil paint, his frown growing with each stroke. The color was all wrong! Or perhaps it was the depth he had seen in those eyes. They had been so clear, he felt he could see straight into her soul.

When Sir Neville's stomach began growling, he looked up in surprise. The sunlight was almost gone, and someone had lit a lamp behind him. He studied his efforts and grimaced, throwing the sketch pad onto the table.

"I'll just have to see those eyes again," he said, a smile spreading slowly across his lips at the thought.

In retrospect, he could recall much more than those startlingly beautiful eyes. The woman had been a beauty, from head to toe. He wondered briefly about companions: did they ever indulge in dalliances with men? Most companions and governesses of his experience were Friday-faced spinsters—most unappealing! But this one! Ah, perhaps he should seek her out again and discover what a ladies' companion did when away from her charges.

Chapter Two

Crisp and cool, thought Neville, stroking the neck of his gray mare. A perfect morning for an early ride in the park. But as he entered the gates, he pulled up on the reins and sat back, studying the numerous nannies and children dotting what should have been the pastoral setting in Green Park.

"Not early enough," he muttered, kicking his mare's sides and riding farther until there was no one about. He gave his horse its head, and they cantered down a narrow bridlepath.

Suddenly the horse shied and planted her feet firmly in the soft earth. Caught unaware, Sir Neville slid forward, his momentum carrying him to the horse's neck before he, too, stopped.

"What the devil is the matter with you, Linda?" he demanded of the mare.

"I beg your pardon," said a familiar voice from the bushes at his side.

Neville kicked his feet free of the stirrups and slid to

the ground. Moving a low-hanging branch, he reached inside and dragged out the governess from the day before, a streak of dirt across her brow. He hardly recognized her, dressed as she was in an old gown covered by an immense cloak. She held a large basket full of flowers which she had evidently pulled out by their roots. Her hair was tied up in a kerchief and covered by one of the ugliest coal-scuttle bonnets he had ever seen, throwing her entire face into shadows. He let go of her immediately.

"What the devil are you doing lurking about in the bushes and startling horses and riders?"

"I was doing no such thing!" intoned Lady Annabelle Fairfax haughtily, showing him her basket. She stole a quick look at his face before she bent her head, refusing to meet his gaze. Mumbling, she added humbly, "I was gathering wildflowers. They are so few and far between in London; one must search everywhere."

"You very nearly had me catapulted into tomorrow!" he said crossly. "Didn't you hear me coming?"

"If I had, sir, I would have hidden myself much more thoroughly! Now, if you will excuse me."

Neville had been brave as long as he could; after slamming into the pommel of his saddle, he wanted to do nothing so much as to rub the inside of his throbbing thighs in a manner no gentleman could do in front of a lady, so he stepped to one side and let her pass. The branch clawed at her skirt, giving Sir Neville another glimpse of that trim ankle. The dowd gave the skirt a quick tug, and there was the sound of fabric tearing. Mortified, she hurried away, leaving behind the bottom half of her petticoat.

Sir Neville grinned and picked up the snowy muslin and lace. It was of excellent quality. She might be a governess, but she was doing quite well for herself.

* * *

"I knew nothing good could come of sitting over a bunch of weeds all afternoon. And here you are, prostrate with the headache, and all because of this nonsensical need to paint things."

"I was trying to draw those flowers, Margaret, not paint them," said Annabelle.

"I still say there's no need to go scrambling all over the place, digging things up, getting all dirty," grumbled Lady Margaret, plumping up the cushions behind her friend's head. "You should have had one of the footmen do that. Or better still, we have lovely flowers in our garden just waiting to be painted!"

"I know, Margaret, I'm sorry."

"Well, it's not for me to correct you, Annabelle, but it simply isn't done, walking all over London, without so much as a maid, and wearing the housekeeper's oldest cloak and bonnet, too."

"Would you rather have had people recognize me?" asked Annabelle, remembering her encounter with the arrogant man from the Royal Academy. It was a shame he was overbearing; he could have been quite handsome. As it was, she was fast developing an aversion for the man.

"Never mind, my dear. You just stay home and rest," said her friend.

"I feel so bad not going with you tonight, Margaret. I never have the headache!"

"Well, I do, and I know the agony you must be feeling. Never fear, I'll take care of our girls. And to be truthful, I think it best I'm not at home tonight. It always goes badly, Harold says, when you mix females and politics."

"I don't see how he can say so, Mama. What does he think last night was? I've never been so bored in all my life playing silver loo with those two cronies of Papa's all night.''

"Charlotte! How can you call Mr. Andrews and Lord Oglethorpe boring! I chose them especially for your table. Why, Mr. Andrews is a charming gentleman, and quite smitten by you, or I miss my guess. You would do well to encourage that young man.''

"Young man? Mama, he must be close to your age! Five and thirty if he's a day!'' complained Charlotte.

"Margaret, please . . .'' said Lady Annabelle weakly.

"There is nothing wrong with a young miss having a firm, steady hand to guide her, is there, Annabelle?''

"Ladies, I really think we should allow Mother to rest,'' said Phoebe, gently but firmly shepherding her hostess and friend out of her mother's sitting room.

"Thank you, dear,'' said Annabelle, closing her eyes.

"You're welcome. Are you really quite well, Mother?''

"Of course, dear. Just a headache. You run along to Lady Oglethorpe's musicale; I'll be fine.''

"If you're certain,'' said Phoebe doubtfully.

"I'm only certain that if I spend much more time listening to inane gossips, I'll go stark raving mad, my dear child,'' said Annabelle, looking fondly at her daughter.

"But Mother, surely you aren't thinking of going home so soon!''

"No, but how I would love an hour of intelligent conversation with a rational person who thinks about more than fashions and the latest *on-dit*. I was raised in the country, Phoebe. I've lived there all my life, and I have been very happy. I hope, though I don't presume to know your mind completely, that someday you, too, will be content with a country life.'' Annabelle stretched out her arm and took her daughter's hand. "It is so much more satisfying than life here in London where the most serious decisions concern what type of lace to use on a new gown.''

"I suppose living in the country will be fine when I am old, Mother, but right now, I want to see everything—do everything," said Phoebe, her enthusiasm contagious.

Annabelle smiled, forgetting her headache at the joy of watching her beautiful titian-haired daughter pirouette around the room.

"You know, Mother, perhaps you could find yourself a husband while you are here. Then you wouldn't have to be alone in the country after I am wed."

"A husband! Me? No, I thank you, my love; it is your turn to shine. I am content to sit with the chaperons and watch your triumphs. Speaking of which, it is time for you to dress. Come back when you are done and show me how you look."

"Yes, Mother," said Phoebe, blowing her parent a kiss before curtseying to an imaginary beau and waltzing out of the room.

With a sigh, Annabelle picked up the miniature of her late husband that always sat by her bed. She studied the strong jaw so like her daughter's.

"Cyril, I wish you were here to see our Phoebe. I wish you could know her." With a slight frown, Annabelle replaced the picture and closed her eyes, murmuring, "And I wish I could remember what it was like when you were with me. It has been so long; were it not for this miniature—which is only a poor likeness—I would not even be able to recall your face."

Unbidden, another man came to mind, and Annabelle tried to frown away the angular face with its bewitching gray eyes, and the dark hair turning to silver at the temples. Why was the face of this maddening man so much easier to bring to mind than her late husband's?

Annabelle greeted the maid's entrance with relief; she was not going to delve into such puzzles tonight!

"I've brought some milk, my lady, with just a drop of laudanum to soothe you," said Mary, entering with a tray.

"Thank you, Mary. Hopefully, it will help me sleep," said Annabelle, not wanting to face the fact that the man from the art museum might have the power to disturb her sleep.

Lady Oglethorpe's musicales were always well attended. It was not so much because of the entertainment, but the fact that the champagne flowed freely, and the buffet tables fairly groaned with the weight of the food.

Phoebe unfurled her fan and whispered behind it, "I don't think there's anyone less than fifty in attendance tonight."

"You're wrong. Mr. Andrews is here; I just saw him. I hope he doesn't spot us," said Charlotte.

"Spot you, you mean. I hold no allure for the politically ambitious Mr. Andrews. He's only looking for a political hostess. I am too flambouyant; I heard him tell your father so."

Trying to slump down in her chair, Charlotte missed the entrance of Sir Neville and his current flirt, Lady Rand-Smythe. But Phoebe detected him immediately.

"Charlotte, over there by that woman. That's him! Don't look, stupid!" hissed Phoebe.

"How am I to know which 'he' you're talking about if I don't look?" whispered Charlotte, the dreaded Mr. Andrews forgotten for the moment. "You're right! It is him, from the other day at the museum. Oh, I wish I could be invisible!"

"You aren't, so we might as well brazen it out," said Phoebe.

"He has seen us," gasped Charlotte, turning her back on Phoebe. "He's staring at us, and that woman beside him has a quizzing glass on us! What if he tells everyone . . ."

Ignoring her friend, Phoebe lifted her chin and stared haughtily at the man and his companion. With a curt nod, he acknowledged her before turning away. He said something to his scantily gowned friend, and she let her quizzing glass fall, laughing as she took his arm and moved away.

Phoebe glared at the pair, saying, "They have gone, Charlotte. You may sit up again."

Charlotte breathed a deep sigh of relief and straightened. Too late did she see the dreaded Mr. Andrews bearing down on them.

"It needed only this," she muttered. "Why, good evening, Mr. Andrews. I had no idea you were a music enthusiast."

"Good evening, Miss Sweet. And Miss Fairfax. May I?" he asked, settling his slight form on the vacant chair next to Charlotte. "Actually, I am not much of an enthusiast; however, I must confess I found out a certain young lady would be attending, and I could not resist!" He smiled at Charlotte coyly.

Charlotte slid a quick glance at her friend and brayed, "Why, Mr. Andrews, you naughty, naughty man! To be saying such outrageous things to such an innocent as I!" With her fan, she gave his forearm a loud rap.

Rubbing his arm, Mr. Andrews looked to the left and right, blinked an uncomfortable smile, and stood up. Sketching a lightning bow, he hurried away.

"Why, whatever was the matter with Mr. Andrews, I wonder?" said Charlotte, hiding behind her fan.

Appearing suddenly at her daughter's side, Lady Sweet whispered, "Charlotte, we will have words when we return home."

"Whew! I thought she would never have done! Phoebe, we simply must think of something to throw my mother off the scent," said Charlotte, flopping inelegantly onto Phoebe's bed. "A solid hour spent listening to 'your duty to your father,' and 'what about your four sisters.' All I want to do is enjoy my first Season! I can find a husband next year! Or if they think I'm going to settle for some dull widower whose only topic of conversation is politics, I can wait several years!" She began taking the pins out of her hair, and it fell in dusky ringlets about her shoulders.

"I wanted to cut all this off, you know, and get one of the latest crops like you, but Mama said that was too radical!" mimicked Charlotte. Noticing her tirade was not producing the desired interest, Charlotte nudged her friend.

"What?" asked Phoebe, startled.

"You've not heard a word I've said. Not that it is anything new. Except about my hair; I don't think I had written to you about that."

"Oh, Charlotte. Don't cut your hair. You look so romantic with it down around your shoulders—rather like Guinevere."

"Do you think so, really?" said Charlotte, bouncing off the bed and going to stand in front of the chevil glass. "You know what would really shock Mama? If I fell in love with a poet—a romantic poet like Byron. The only trouble is, I don't think poets frequent political soirees. So where does one find a poet, I wonder?" added Charlotte thoughtfully.

Phoebe laughed. "You would probably have to go to one of those deadly boring literary salons. Then everyone would think you a bluestocking, and no gentleman would ever want to marry you!"

"That would be fine with me if it only lasted a year or two. Really, Phoebe, why would either of us want to marry so quickly? Having a husband telling me I should stay home instead of go to Lady Thingamy's ball isn't at all appealing."

"But what if you could control the husband?" mused Phoebe.

"Can it be done?" asked Charlotte, her mouth turning down petulantly. "In my experience, the wives are always doing as they are bid. I'm not sure I can be so docile. Mama says I am quite spoiled, and I suppose there is a grain of truth in that since Papa allows me anything I want. But he doesn't mind, truly he doesn't. Giving me things makes him happy, too. And I never, or at least rarely, have a tantrum."

"That is because he always lets you have your way. You must find a husband who would treat you the same way!" said Phoebe, nodding to herself at this sensible thought. "Just look at my mother. Why, she's quite comfortable telling me what to do. I can't imagine her ever submitting to some husband. Not that she had to for very long since my father passed away only six months after they were wed."

"What will she do when you are no longer there to order about?" asked Charlotte, intrigued.

"I hadn't really thought about it before, and neither has she, or I miss my bet. If she had, then why would she be talking about finding a husband for me so soon? That's all I've heard for the past year. 'When we get to London . . . we'll find you a husband.' You know, if I want a husband, I'll find him, but I really just want to go to balls and routs and breakfasts until I drop. And of course, there is our other list to complete. We haven't even been to Parliament yet."

"I know what you mean, but my mother is so anxious for me to be wed. Next year, there will be the twins to launch."

"But why should you be sacrificed for them?" demanded Phoebe.

"Exactly! They are rushing both of us, and we shouldn't allow it!" exclaimed Charlotte, sitting up and facing Phoebe.

"So how do we foil their plans?" whispered Phoebe, her brow rising like her mother's did. "They won't all be as easy as your Mr. Andrews. And besides, some of them have no designs on marriage; Goodie and West are too much fun to discourage."

"True. We'll just have to study each situation and each suitor individually. Then we'll know what to do to give each one a disgust of us—without crossing the lines of propriety. I've no desire to be locked up on bread and water like I was when we were sent home from school for—"

Giggles erupted.

"Miss May let us come back, but she never did forgive us," said Charlotte finally.

"Can you blame her? Thinking she had a secret admirer and then having her hopes dashed?"

"I suppose it was rather bad of us," said Charlotte.

"No more than she deserved after humiliating you in front of the entire school!" returned Phoebe, her eyes flashing with angry memories.

Charlotte patted her hand. "Don't worry about it. Now, back to our plan."

"It isn't so very difficult discouraging gentlemen."

"How do you know?" demanded Charlotte.

"Oh, I had to depress Tony Gilbreath at home," said Phoebe with an airy wave of her hand.

Bouncing on the bed and tugging at Phoebe's sleeve, Charlotte said, "Not Terrible Tony! Oh, do tell!"

"It was last fall, the night of the Harvest Festival. Mama said I might dance, and Tony stood up with me for the quadrille. Each time the dance brought us together, he squeezed my hand in such a familiar way. And then ..." Phoebe, a natural actress, paused for effect and glanced around the empty chamber. "He took me outside and kissed me!"

"Where?"

"On the lips of course!"

"Oh, Phoebe! That was rather fast of you to allow him such a liberty!"

Phoebe shrugged and said haughtily, "I didn't allow him. I slapped his face so hard he had to leave by way of the darkened garden!"

"Ooh!" breathed Charlotte, falling into a thoughtful silence. Finally, she asked quietly, "What was it like?"

"Quite pleasant, really, though I never let him know it! But it could be used as a weapon to discourage unwanted suitors."

Charlotte frowned. "How?"

"For a small *pourboire*, I'm sure a handsome footman would agree to give one a kiss."

"Oh my goodness!" exclaimed Charlotte, truly appalled at her friend's outrageous suggestion.

"Don't you see? If someone like Mr. Andrews were to witness such an act, he would certainly reconsider courting you. Yet, being an honorable sort, he couldn't very well tell your mother what you had been up to." concluded Phoebe, quite pleased with her logic.

"But what if he were to punch the footman in the nose?"

"Well, then we would need to pay the footman a bonus or something," said Phoebe dismissively.

"Hm. It seems a sound plan."

"The main thing is to keep our mothers from finding out—especially *my* mother." Phoebe lay back and stared up at the heavy bed curtains thoughtfully. Turning on her side, she looked up at Charlotte and said, "What do you think I should do about my mother? She is much too sharp-witted. Not that your mother is not, Charlotte, but mine keeps a much closer eye on me than your mother does on you, and I don't think I could fool her for long if I tried to discourage every suitor who looked my way. Nor am I sure I want to! I do want to enjoy my Season!"

"True, true. Perhaps you can think of some way to distract her if you should need to discourage a particularly persistent beau."

"Hmm. What she needs is something to distract her . . ." Phoebe sat straight up and clapped her hands together. "That's it! I'll turn the tables on her! While she thinks I'm here to find a husband, I'll be looking for one for her!"

"Ingenious!"

"She has enough of a fortune to attract one," said Phoebe, mentally ticking off her mother's marriageability quotient. "And she is still young enough to attract a mature man."

"She's still quite pretty, really," said Charlotte charitably.

"Well, she'll do, I suppose," said Phoebe. "And she likes children. We might find a widower seeking a mother for his children."

"I don't know about that. Then you would have half brothers or sisters, and I can tell you from experience with my own full sisters, it is *not* pleasant!"

"Well, perhaps only one or two children. But with any luck, she'll be so busy being courted during this Season, we won't have to worry about her looking over our shoulders all the time. I daresay I might last two or three Seasons before I need settle down."

"All I care about is this one. As you said, your mother is much too observant!" Charlotte agreed, saying, "What's more, we should even be able to go on all of our adventures without worrying so about your mother's eagle eye!"

"Then it's settled!" exclaimed Phoebe, clapping her hands together gleefully. "First thing tomorrow, we start looking for a husband for my mother!"

Chapter Three

"So this is Almack's?" murmured Phoebe as they crossed the threshold.

"Almack's," breathed Charlotte, suitably impressed.

"Hmph," sniffed Phoebe.

"Phoebe, please remember, it is the Society here which can make or break your Season," warned her mother.

Phoebe gave a brilliant smile, unwittingly causing a number of gentlemen present to neglect their present partners while they studied this new beauty.

"Mother, I assure you, I shan't forget anything. Look, Charlotte, here comes Goodie."

The tall, redheaded young man bowed over each lady's hand before turning to Charlotte. "They are playing a waltz next, Miss Sweet. Have you permission yet?"

"No, not yet, but I would love some refreshments. The evening is so unseasonably warm," said Charlotte, taking his proffered arm.

"Now, that was prettily done," said Lady Annabelle, nodding toward the retreating couple.

"Yes, Mother," said Phoebe, her green eyes wide and innocent.

"Well, there are times, Phoebe, when you could learn a thing or two from my Charlotte," put in Lady Margaret. "And since she is accustomed to living here in London so much of the year and attending my little suppers . . ."

"Margaret, isn't that the most dreadful gown Lady Osgood has chosen," whispered Lady Annabelle, successfully diverting her friend from a boring lecture about social graces which would only try Phoebe's patience, not to mention her own.

Phoebe nodded a silent thanks to her mother before turning to the approaching gentleman with a welcoming smile. "Ah, good evening, Lord Forbes."

"Good evening Lady Sweet, Lady Fairfax, Miss Fairfax. Might I procure some orangeat for you ladies?"

"Not for us, thank you, my lord. But perhaps Phoebe would enjoy a glass?" said Lady Annabelle.

"Miss Fairfax?"

"Why, yes, my lord. I would love some."

When they had departed, Annabelle looked around the glittering ballroom for familiar faces. Since arriving in London, she had renewed a number of acquaintances from her days at Miss Brown's Seminary for Young Ladies. Having married out of the schoolroom, Annabelle had not kept up with her old friends, except Margaret. Her old "friends" had exclaimed upon seeing her, had sympathized with her exile, and had provided countless invitations to help her "make up for lost time."

Had anyone bothered to ask, Annabelle would have informed them that she hadn't been rusticating, nor had she been pining for the gay life. She had been imminently content with her life, running the profitable estate her late husband had provided for her and their beautiful daughter and watching Phoebe grow up. Annabelle hadn't had time to mourn what might have been.

No one asked, of course, and when she suddenly appeared, dressed in the first stare of fashion, looking much younger than many of her more jaded friends, they hid their annoyance because, after all, Annabelle was such a dear lady. Everyone loved her.

Tonight she wore a silk gown of Prussian blue, its high waist lending height to her slender form; the décolletage was much too low, although the dressmaker had labeled it modest. Her hair was hidden by a matronly turban which Margaret assured her was all the crack. Around her neck was a magnificent sapphire nestled in a circlet of diamonds. Matching bracelets were on each wrist, and a sapphire broach held the turban in place. The dark color of the gown emphasized her creamy skin, and allowed her eyes to be the bright focal point of her appearance. She was, in short, beautiful.

Left to her own devices while Margaret conversed with another politician's wife, Annabelle tapped her foot as the dancers whirled around the floor. The waltz was an energetic dance, she mused, and except for the fact that one's partner practically embraced one, it looked like it would be very exciting. Her mind wandered to the last time anyone, any man, had placed a hand on her waist. Ah well, the waltz was not for her. She was content with her role as duenna. She had no intention of indulging in such a frivolous pastime as dancing. That was for the young ladies.

Sir Neville Colston pushed away from the pillar he was holding up and stared in a most ungentlemanly manner at the turbaned woman directly across the dance floor. Each glimpse he caught of her between the waltzing figures intrigued him; he had seen her before. But surely he wouldn't have forgotten that trim figure, he thought. The hair was covered, of course, but her breasts, her neck, that strong chin, those . . .

Those eyes! After seeing her in the park with that dreadful bonnet, he had all but forgotten those incredible eyes!

Neville started forward only to be caught up by the dancers. Hastily, he backed out of the melee and threaded his way around the twirling couples. Not ten feet from her he stopped, watching her changing expressions as she followed the movements of the dance. Her eyes were just as bewitching as he remembered from the museum. She really was a puzzle; he could have sworn she was only some mousy little governess. But there couldn't be a governess at Almack's. Even if she were a paid companion, she wouldn't be dressed so richly.

Then Neville noticed her toe tapping, and a lazy smile spread across his face, erasing his usual cynical expression with amusement. He stepped forward, dipped a hasty bow, took her hand, and quickly moved into the midst of the dancers. His startled partner had no choice but to remain in his arms and try to follow his lead.

"What do you think . . . You again!" exclaimed Annabelle in a furious whisper.

"Yes, me!" he said, laughing at her.

She tried to pull away. "Let . . . go . . . of . . . me!" she hissed, removing his hand from her waist only to have it return each time holding her closer still.

"I'm afraid that would be most unwise, Miss . . ."

Annabelle's lips pursed angrily, and her left brow shot heavenward.

Her forbidding stare had no effect on Sir Neville, and he teased, "You may as well tell me. I'll find out anyway; we seem destined to keep company together."

"Lady Annabelle Fairfax."

"My lady, I beg your pardon. I had guessed you were the governess or a paid companion, perhaps," he said, giving the semblance of a bow even as they continued to dance. "And I am Sir Neville Colston, at your service, my lady."

"Were you truly at my service, Sir Neville, you would defend me against ruffians who steal dances without so much as a by-your-leave!"

"What? Shall I slay myself? And had I asked, my dear Lady Annabelle, you would have cut my heart out with a refusal."

"Then you, sir, would have died happily for the pleasure of serving me."

"Touché," said Sir Neville, taking the hand he held and bringing it to his lips for a daring kiss. Annabelle gasped and missed her step, but his strong arms saved her, guiding her back into rhythm with him.

Annabelle silently cursed her wretched thoughts about a man's hand at her waist; somehow, she had conjured up this maddening, insulting man. But his hand seemed to burn into her skin, and she wondered wildly how a stranger's touch could discomfit her so.

"Ahem."

Annabelle looked from his snowy cravat to his gray eyes, which were crinkling with amusement.

"Yes?" she snapped, not wanting to encourage him.

"You do waltz divinely, my dear Lady Annabelle."

"I must remind you, sir, that I am not your dear anything!"

"Perhaps. Only time will tell, but I feel I must tell you, although I hesitate to say anything, that it is customary for the gentleman to lead—though you do lead quite well.''

"Oh! I . . . I do beg your pardon!''

A blush rose delightfully, stealing its way to her cheeks; Sir Neville caught his breath. How could he have thought her plain, even wearing the ugliest bonnet ever devised.

"Think nothing of it,'' he managed to say, feeling as tongue-tied as a schoolboy.

"It is because of my daughter, you see.''

"Your daughter? Not one of those,'' he faltered, but finished gallantly, "young ladies from the Royal Academy?''

"Yes, Phoebe.''

"The red-haired one,'' said Sir Neville. "My condolences.''

Annabelle's eyes blazed, and she closed her mouth.

After a moment spent admiring her strong profile while she stared into space, Neville laughed. "Peace, peace. I was being boorish. Come, you must forgive me; I am unaccustomed to being around children, especially young ladies. I am an uncle five times over, but they are all boys, you see.''

Annabelle thawed minutely. "Apology accepted.''

"Good. Now, will you please explain why your beautiful daughter could be the cause of your trying to lead.''

Annabelle knew she owed him nothing, certainly not civility. Hadn't he practically kidnapped her for this waltz? Trying to harden her heart against him, she made the mistake of looking into his laughing eyes.

Annabelle answered with a ready smile and said, "At home, there was no one for her to practice with, and I said I would . . . would dance with her, playing the part of the gentleman.''

"A difficult role, indeed, for one of your great beauty," said Sir Neville, once more on familiar footing.

But Annabelle wasn't impressed by his smooth response, her smile fading even as the music did. Ignoring his proffered arm, she glared at him and snapped, "Fustian!"

He took her hand again, but Annabelle pulled free of his grasp and hurried away, asking the first servant for the location of the ladies withdrawing room. Having reached its privacy, Annabelle took out a handkerchief and dipped it in the pitcher of cool water to mop her face.

How dare he! Sir Neville, indeed! He was nothing but an interloper who dealt in Spanish coin! First there was the insult to both her and the girls at the Royal Academy! Then his incivility in the park! And now this! Stealing a dance with her! Not just a dance, she corrected—a waltz! Her first waltz! Very probably her only waltz! She would never forgive him!

"Mother? Are you feeling all right?"

"I'm fine. I just got a little overheated, that's all," she replied, looking up to find Phoebe staring at her with open curiosity.

"I didn't know you planned to dance," said Phoebe, her voice coy and teasing.

"No more did I," she said.

"Who is that odious man?"

"Never mind. Oh, isn't that the quadrille? We should be getting back; you don't want to disappoint your partner."

Annabelle pushed past her thoughtful daughter and made her way back to the chaperons, taking a seat in the middle of several gossiping matrons.

There! she thought. That should effectively spike his guns should he feel tempted to assault her again!

But Annabelle needn't have worried. Sir Neville, after his single dance with her, turned to his usual amusements with Lady Rand-Smythe, soothing her ruffled feathers.

The raven-haired beauty pretended to ignore him when he bowed to her, but the pretense didn't last long, and by the playing of the next waltz, she was leaning into him, her exposed breasts affording him a pleasant view.

Lady Annabelle tried to concentrate on the gossip swirling around her, but much to her dismay, her eyes kept betraying her, searching the crowd as if they had a mind of their own. Her inattentiveness was noticed by the sharp-eyed matrons, and they exchanged speaking glances over the top of her too-pretty head.

Lady Rand-Smythe fairly purred when Sir Neville procured some weak tea and secretly poured a dollop of brandy in each cup.

With a leer, she said, "You always add that little extra something to the evening."

"Your wish is my command, my lady. My only pleasure is to—"

An overly loud trill of laughter made heads turn and brows lift as if to say, "What sort of sound is that to rent the stale night air at Almack's?"

"What the deuce . . ." muttered Sir Neville, looking up with a frown. "I might have known."

"Known? Are those girls acquaintances of yours?" asked Lady Rand-Smyth haughtily. "Oh yes, they were at the musicale. But you never told me how you made their acaquaintances."

"I met them briefly the other day, but I don't even know their names." He detected the flicker of displeasure in her dark eyes and added gallantly, "Nor do I wish to. Not when I have you by my side."

She sighed with contentment. "Some schoolroom misses up from the country, no doubt." Then she set about amusing and teasing him so he had no time or thought for anything else.

"Let's get away from here," he said, his voice impatient.

The laugh that followed never rose above the voluptuous widow's throat. She tucked her hand into the crook of his arm and allowed him to propel her toward the hallowed portals of Almack's and onto the street.

"This is much better," she said, "away from all those noisy people."

"Personally, I think anyone under the age of thirty should be banned from Almack's," said Sir Neville, looking over his shoulder. " 'Twould be a much more pleasant haunt."

Camilla rapped him playfully on the arm and cast him a coy look. "But my dear Neville, then I wouldn't be allowed in to dance with you."

He ignored the hint of crow's feet at the corners of her dark eyes and said, "Oh, very well, Camilla. No one under the age of two and twenty."

She patted his hand and pressed her bosom against his arm most shamelessly.

"Ah," she whispered, "if only you hadn't gone off to fight Napoleon, perhaps I might now be Lady Colston instead of a poor widow."

Sir Neville Colston knew very well the response she wished to hear, but a devilishly perverse streak bade him remain silent, and her hint passed awkwardly between them. It was that same streak of self-preservation which had allowed him to escape wedded bliss for seven and thirty years, despite his most eligible bachelor state. And of late, Camilla's hints that he make their satisfying relationship more permanent had begun to weary him.

When they arrived at Camilla's home, Neville walked her up the steps, bowing deeply over her hand but declining to enter and enjoy her offer of, "uh, refreshments."

With a jaunty step, Neville made his way back to his club, where he found a number of friends already engrossed in a game of faro. This is much better, he thought, just a group of friends; no need for pretense here.

"Hullo, Nev. Thought you were squiring the divine Camilla around t'night," said Sinbad Sinclair, an old army friend. "Almack's, supper at Grillon's, and"—Sinclair paused for effect and winked, adding—"and all that. We expect to read your names in the paper any day now."

"Not today, old friend, and not tonight. No, I thought I would rather repair my finances by joining you at the tables. It's a good thing I didn't leave it until later; there might have been nothing left to win from you."

The assembled company laughed at this quip even as Mr. Sinclair's fair complexion turned a ruddy color. But the younger man joined in the laughter and issued a ludicrous challenge to his friend.

"By tomorrow, Nev, I'll own that estate of yours in the wilds of Cornwall," said the younger man.

"Time will tell, Sinbad, only time will tell."

Sir Neville rarely sat through the night at White's; with his devilish good luck, acknowledged one opponent, he had no need to wear himself out. This night was no exception. However, since he could not persuade his friend to leave with him, Neville merely went back to his house near Grosvenor, breakfasted, and changed into fresh linens, happily discarding the knee breeches which were *de rigueur* at Almack's.

Then he returned to White's and sought out his friend, who was still sitting at the faro table, alone now.

"Hand cramped?" asked Neville quietly.

"What's that supposed to mean?"

"Thought your hand might be cramped from scribbling vowels."

"I didn't do that badly!" said the small man, glaring petulantly at his tall, lanky friend. "Not after you left," he added with his usual crooked grin.

"Good! By the way, old chap, I've brought my team and sent for yours."

"Your team?" echoed Sinclair, frowning mightily as he tried to recall the import of this statement.

"You remember! That bet we made last night," said Neville. "Well, if you were too drunk to recall, I don't suppose I can hold you to it." With that, Neville started out the door.

On the steps of White's, his friend caught him up and demanded, "Once again now, what exactly are the terms of this wager, Nev?"

Sir Neville suppressed a grin, knowing full well that Sinclair could not know the terms since they had never made such a bet. But he answered smoothly, "That my man can harness a team faster than yours."

"Done!" croaked Sinclair, hurrying down the steps to confer with his tiger.

Sir Neville watched with a slight twitch of his lips. A raised brow and a simple nod prepared his own tiger, who tightened his grip on the horses' lead ropes.

"You'll start them, Maltby. Right?"

The obedient batman nodded solemnly and descended the steps of White's. Behind Sir Neville and Mr. Sinclair stood half the early morning occupants of White's, most still clad in their rumpled evening dress from the past night's revels. Betting books were scribbled in hastily as Maltby raised his white handkerchief.

"One . . . two . . . three!"

A shout went up from the spectators as the scrap of cloth fluttered to the ground. Mr. Sinclair's docile cattle stood stock-still. Sir Neville's restive team took instant exception to the foreign object floating before them and began to plunge and rear, dragging the small tiger to and fro.

"Hah! I've got you now, Nev! Look at m' tiger go! It looks like your man will be lucky if he doesn't have to chase your beasts all the way to Richmond!"

"Yes, you have me there," said Sir Neville, languidly moving down the steps. He looked beyond his harassed tiger and batman, beyond his rearing horses, and noted that his friend's groom was well on the way to finishing his job.

"Easy, easy boys," he said quietly. The horses' ears pricked forward, and they stood still, almost at attention. He stroked their gray-velvet noses while his tiger, muttering under his breath in Spanish, released their lead ropes and quickly harnessed the now-quiet team.

"That was five hundred, correct?" said Sir Neville, taking out his purse as he joined his friend by the steps.

"That's right," said Sinclair, suddenly looking uneasy. "I say, Nev, you didn't just let me win, just because I lost at faro all night."

"As if I would!" said the imperturbable veteran. "No, you made the bet fair and square; it was a race between our tigers. Now, if it had been you and I—"

"I'm not that drunk!" laughed his friend, feeling once again at ease.

"So much the worse for me," laughed Neville, clapping Sinclair on the back.

Sir Neville saw his friend drive off before he turned

his team toward the stables. This was really getting to be a drain on his patience, he thought. Perhaps not *his* patience, but certainly on his hot-tempered tiger, Antonio, and his former batman, Maltby. This was the third time this quarter he'd had to reinforce Sinclair's sagging finances. He would simply have to tell his friend . . .

But no, that wouldn't work; Sinclair's pride was such that he'd probably go out and put a bullet in his head like old Formby had done when he'd lost his estate to Neville. The last thing he wanted was to lose another friend.

When they reached the house, Neville let Maltby out and said, "Tell Peters I'll want a bath drawn at precisely two o'clock."

"Aye, major. And your phaeton with your drawing case in it at the front door at half past."

Neville shook his head and frowned sternly at his former batman, now servant and secretary. "Am I grown so predictable?"

"No, sir. Th' cook still sets his clock by Big Ben. But th' rest of this lot of soft city servants figure when to be seen working by your comings and goings. It's Thursday so you must be going to that museum."

"I suppose I'll just have to shake things up a bit."

"What? Have your bath drawn at half past instead of two on th' dot? Why, whatever would the neighbors think?"

"Enough of your surliness. Just do as you're told," grumbled Neville.

"Aye, aye, sir."

"How do I look," said Charlotte, settling her rakish hat on her smooth hair.

Walking around her friend, Phoebe finally nodded. "You'll do, Charlie," she said.

Charlotte giggled and asked, "You can't tell I've got long hair?"

"No, not with that high shirt collar."

"I hope Papa doesn't miss all of this. It was hard enough getting into his rooms without his man noticing us. I don't want to have to put it all back!"

"Probably better if we don't try. Besides, we'll need them again," said Phoebe, looking in the mirror and shaking her head. "I do wish I didn't have red hair. My complexion is so fair; I look positively feminine."

This struck Charlotte as being inordinately funny, and it was several minutes before Phoebe could ask, "Will I do?"

"I think so. Come on, we better go," said Charlotte. "I do hope you're not tempted to bid on a horse. We cannot possibly pass for gentlemen if we are closely scrutinized."

"I won't. I promise."

But Phoebe's promise was quickly tested once they set foot in Tattersall's. The famous auction house for horses consisted of an enclosed paddock with a glass roof to protect the bidders from the weather. Ladies never attended.

"Charlie," Phoebe whispered to her friend. "I've simply got to have this one. Look at her coat! She's the same color as my hair! On her, just think what a dash I could cut in the park!"

"Phillip, you promised," groaned Charlotte.

"But Charlie, she's too perfect! And going for a song, too. Just look at that confirmation!"

"You'll never get away with it!"

"Just watch!" said Phoebe, stepping closer to the ring.

Her raised hand was crushed in an iron grip and brought to her side.

"Was that a bid, sir?" asked the auctioneer.

"No," called the man holding her hand.

Phoebe looked around sharply and found herself nose to nose with the man who had harassed them at the museum and had waltzed with her mother.

"You!" she breathed, her eyes flashing.

Neville grinned. "Yes, me, and you will thank me, minx."

"Not unless I get that mare," she whispered.

He threw her a warning glance and jerked his head toward the spot where Charlotte waited, frozen with fear.

"I'm selling this mare for the last time," said the auctioneer. Sir Neville raised his hand, and the bid rose higher.

"You will leave immediately, Miss Fairfax. And you, I assume, are the partner in crime," he said, nodding to Charlotte.

"And for the last time . . ."

Sir Neville raised his hand again, and the bid rose again. "I want both of you out of here. I'll call later."

"Sold to Sir Neville Colston."

Phoebe almost squealed with delight, but his fierce frown quelled her excitement. With a flash of a smile, the two girls left Tattersall's, undetected and happy.

Phoebe and Charlotte, alias Charlie and Phillip, hurried away. They hailed a hackney cab for their journey home and had the driver deliver them to the stables near the house. Making their way through the fragrant garden to the morning room, they slipped inside and stole up the backstairs to the safety of Phoebe's room.

"Good morning . . . girls?" said Annabelle, looking them up and down.

With a gasp, they whirled to face her. Seated at the window in the morning sun, they hadn't noticed her when they entered the room. Now, however, they could see she was comfortably ensconced on the window seat, her embroidery in hand as if she had been there for some time.

"Mother, we can explain . . ."

"Lady Annabelle, this is not what it looks like."

"Isn't it? You know, I was most intrigued—no, almost frightened—when I saw two strange young men leaving the house by way of the garden early this morning. And then I noticed how one was tall and thin and the other rather short and slight. So, I checked your beds and found you had already gone out. I would like to say that I felt much more easy about those strange young men, but such wasn't the case. You can understand my concern, ladies," said Annabelle, her lips curling slightly.

"We just wanted to go out on our own," said Phoebe, gazing at the floor. "And we felt that, dressed as we are, it would cause less comment."

"I see. And is that the story you wish to tell, Charlotte?"

"I . . . yes, my lady," said Charlotte, hanging her head.

"I see."

"You're not going to tell my mother, are you?"

Lady Annabelle rose and smoothed her skirts. "No, I'm not. Your mother has been called away and is packing even as we speak."

"Called away? What has happened?"

"Two of your sisters have contracted the chicken pox. And their governess has also succumbed to it."

"Oh, then it's not too serious," said Charlotte.

"No, everyone will recover," said Annabelle, strolling around behind the girls for a different view. "If you wish to say goodbye to her without causing her to have the apoplexy, you might want to change out of those clothes."

"Oh, yes, my lady! Immediately!" said Charlotte, hurrying through the door to the adjoining dressing room.

"I should change, too, Mother," said Phoebe, starting to remove her cravat.

"Not too shabby a job on that cravat," said her mother. "It's a waterfall, isn't it."

Phoebe smiled and nodded.

"Phoebe, this can't go on. You cannot continue to flaunt society's rules and hope to have your reputation remain intact."

"No one recognized us," stated her daughter flatly.

"Not this time, but what about the next time when you decide to tie your garters in public."

"Mother! As if I would—"

Annabelle silenced her with one look at her outrageous outfit.

"Change quickly so that we may say goodbye to Lady Margaret." Pausing at the door, Annabelle mused, "You are too old to thrash, not that I ever managed to do that anyway. I believe, however, that I should have plucked up the courage after all."

Chapter Four

Late that afternoon, while Phoebe penned newsy letters to the neighbors back home under the watchful eye of Annabelle, a footman entered and handed her a note.

With a little cry of excitement, Phoebe jumped to her feet and hurried toward the front door.

At the bottom of the steps, a tiger wearing unfamiliar livery was holding the lead rope of the sorrel mare from Tattersall's.

"Oh, she is beautiful!" exclaimed Phoebe.

"*Sí, senorita,* very beautiful."

"But where did it come from?" demanded Annabelle, looking first at the sorrel mare and then at Phoebe.

"I, uh . . . it's a gift."

"A gift? From whom? Who would be sending you such an extravagant gift? Phoebe, the truth now. I will find out sooner or later, you know."

"Very well, it's from Sir Neville Colston."

Annabelle felt as if she'd been struck. "How did

you . . . ? What has he . . . ? How dare he toy with the affections of a young lady!''

She turned on her heel, leaving Phoebe to throw the reins of the mare back to the groom and follow in her mother's wake. Phoebe found her mother already writing busily at the small escritoire in the morning room.

"Mother! What are you doing?"

"I am writing Sir Neville Colston to tell him exactly what I think of a bounder of his age compromising a young lady! He should know better! And he will, when I have done with him! So that's why he wanted to dance with me—to get closer to you!"

"What are you talking about?" But the pen continued to move across the paper. Horror-stricken, Phoebe ripped the missive off the desk and shredded it, crying, "Mother, you really mustn't!"

Annabelle rose and took her daughter's hands, squeezing them tightly. "I know this is difficult for you to understand, sweetheart, but he is completely unsuitable for you. He's handsome and charming, of course, and knows how to turn a pretty phrase, but he's much too sophisticated, too—"

"Old!" Phoebe collapsed on the sofa, prostrate, strangled sounds coming from her, her shoulders shaking.

Annabelle knelt on the floor and put her arm around her daughter's shoulders. "I know it's hard for you now, Phoebe, but someday you'll understand. You'll find someone else, someone more suitable."

Gasping for air, Phoebe struggled to sit up, a stupid smile forming on her lips. She is hysterical, thought Annabelle, her heart breaking for her daughter's pain.

"Mother, Mother, you really have the wrong end of the stick! I promise you, I am not in love with Sir Neville! Why, I barely tolerate the man! He is always interfering with our plans! How he can always happen to be in the wrong place at the wrong time, I have no idea! He is . . ." Phoebe paused, her chagrin over revealing these facts visible on her face. With a sheepish grin, she patted Annabelle's hand and added, "Sir Neville merely purchased the mare for me. I intend to pay him back."

Annabelle sat back on her heels, her narrow gaze and pursed lips warning of her impending outburst.

"Go to your room."

"But Lord West and I were to go riding."

"Never mind that now. Go to your room. And furthermore, we will not be going out this evening. Tell Charlotte, please."

"Yes, Mother," whispered Phoebe, rising and slipping out of the morning room.

Annabelle picked up the shredded note, pouring it from one hand to the other. After a few moments, she rang for Ames, the Sweets' starchy butler, startling him by requesting a hackney cab.

Annabelle pulled her cloak more closely about her as she left the cab and started up the steps to Sir Neville's door. At least, she thought, he has a house and not simply bachelor apartments.

The door opened, and the butler took her calling card, the corner turned down to show she was calling in person. After a glance at the card, he showed her into a formal salon.

"I will inform Sir Neville of your arrival personally, my lady."

"Thank you."

Annabelle wondered momentarily if she had lost her mind, coming to a bachelor's abode. Were she young and unmarried, she would be compromising herself irrevocably. But she was a matron, she reminded herself for the umpteenth time. Such rules didn't apply; still she hoped no one had recognized her as she entered the house. The last thing she could wish was to be thought Sir Neville's paramour. However, she had been careful; there was nothing to worry about, she reassured herself.

So why are there butterflies swarming in my stomach? she asked herself. Certainly the cause couldn't be from seeing Sir Neville Colston again.

Then the door opened, and he stepped into the room, his tall, elegant form dominating the chamber. Annabelle realized she was holding her breath and expelled it audibly. Neville smiled and waved her to the sofa. He joined her, keeping to the opposite end, but Annabelle couldn't ignore his overpowering presence. She shook herself mentally; she had met heads of state since her sojourn at Margaret's house; there was no need to elevate this man to the status of a god. She cleared her throat and faced him.

"I feel certain only an important matter would have brought you here today. What may I do for you, my lady?"

"I have come to ask you not to associate with my daughter, Sir Neville. For some reason, she has formed some sort of attachment to you."

"You mean she fancies me?" he asked, shock and distaste over such a possibility written plainly on his features.

Annabelle grimaced. "No, I don't think that is it, not precisely. It is more fatherly, I believe."

Sir Neville choked and began to cough; obligingly, Annabelle rapped him on the back. Finally, he managed, "Fatherly?"

"So it seems. I thought at first she did fancy you, but

she quickly disabused me of that notion, telling me you were much too old. And I had to believe her; she was most emphatic on the word 'old,' you see. So . . .''

"I understand," he said, his eyes curiously cold.

"Oh! You really mustn't be offended; to a young person, forty is absolutely ancient." Annabelle had the most peculiar whim to pat his hand.

"I am seven and thirty," said Neville.

"Oh . . . oops," said Annabelle, her sardonic smile making his eyes dance as they had done at Almack's. "Well, she told me the most outrageous tale about your buying her a horse . . .''

"I did, at Tattersall's."

"But why on earth—''

"Because she wanted the mare. She obviously has quite an eye for horseflesh; the price was quite reasonable. The bidding was low because the mare was rather small. She will be a perfect mount for your daughter, however, so I thought she should have it."

"But how did you know she wanted it? For that matter, how did she know about the horse being at Tattersall's?" Growing comprehension made Annabelle shiver. "This morning, I caught them sneaking home dressed in . . . They were there, weren't they? Did you help them get into Tattersall's?"

"Certainly not," he snapped. "And as for their presence, it is not my place to answer that, my lady. Let us simply say that everything turned out as it should. Your daughter has a horse imminently suited to her, and I— old thing that I am—I have had the pleasure of playing knight-errant."

"Then you didn't . . . Of course not! I am so embarrassed Sir Neville; I came here to . . . Please accept my apologies, and my daughter's. What you must think of me!'' Annabelle rose and shook his hand quickly before hurrying to the door of the salon.

"Your apology is entirely unnecessary, my dear Anna . . . lady.''

"Oh, but it is. And I assure you, sir, you will not be troubled by either me or my unruly offspring again! Good day.''

Neville started after her, but pulled up short. What could you say? he asked himself. You certainly don't wish to be tangled up in the affairs of such a hoyden, or her mother. Indeed, Neville, old boy, the mother is doubtless more dangerous to your peace of mind and freedom than the daughter!

You are much better off this way!

But doubts lingered when he recalled their waltz and the way her supple body moved in perfect rhythm with his and how her green eyes alternately flashed with fire and then danced with amusement.

Neville shook his head; no doubt about it, Lady Annabelle Fairfax was a dangerous female indeed!

"Devil take you, Sinbad. Why the deuce did you want to come here? The females are dirty, the tables probably crooked, and the brandy will no doubt be unspeakable!'' said Sir Neville, quickly surveying the dark, smoky atmosphere of the Devil's Den, one of the latest gambling hells in Pall Mall.

"I tell you, Nev, Owenby and Pritchard won a fortune here last night. And the night before it was Farrell. I can't help but win, especially if I'm playing against the house and not you!''

"Hello, Sinclair! And Colston, a pleasant surprise to find you here.''

Sir Neville looked over the portly man with the oily mustache and nodded curtly.

"Are you part owner in this, Lansdown?"

"Oh, just a pittance of an interest in it, you know. Of course, it hasn't proven to be the investment I expected," said Lansdown, leaning closer and adding confidentially, "Bloody dealers tend to lose more than they win, you know."

"Is that right," said Sinclair, trying to act nonchalant, but fooling no one. "There's an empty seat over there, Nev. I think I'll just try my hand once or twice."

"We'll find you another chair, Colston."

"Don't bother, Lansdown. I'll just keep an eye on my friend there."

So saying, Neville took up residence leaning against the wall nearest the door of the gaming hell. He accepted a glass of dark liquid from a "hostess," but refused her offer of a cozy chat. His eyes never left the table where Sinclair was playing, but his mind wandered.

I'm getting too old for this, Neville thought, his gaze traveling around the smoky room before coming to rest on his friend. He shook his head. How the deuce does Sinclair, one of the fiercest fighters I ever met in all my years on the Peninsula, as well as the bloody battles at Quatre Bras and Waterloo, still manage to be such a naive lamb waiting for the slaughter? And I'm not much better, he thought, always coming to his rescue. What Sinclair needs is a lady friend. He couldn't get in as much trouble with a nice, safe ladybird in keeping to occupy his hours, mused Neville.

A half-clad female sat down beside his friend, her hand stealing inside his coat as she snuggled against him. Neville pushed off from the wall to glare at her; she sat back and pretended a great interest in the dice.

Neville relaxed. He shook his head, recalling Lady

Annabelle Fairfax's promise to keep away from him. As much trouble as that hoyden daughter had put him through, he should be delighted with her promise. But he wasn't. The prospect of not speaking to Annabelle, not watching her expressive green eyes ... it was unthinkable. And how the devil had he come to that particular state of affairs? he asked himself, trying to frown, but smiling instead as he recalled her last visit. Somehow, he had to make her break that ridiculous promise.

He shifted uncomfortably; each time Annabelle invaded his thoughts, he felt a warmth spread through him such as he had never felt for Camilla. With Camilla, there had been warmth and desire, but mostly in his loins.

In some indefinable manner, Lady Annabelle Fairfax was different. And despite the fact that she might prove dangerous to his bachelor state, he found the idea of not seeing her again intolerable. But she was a woman of great determination, and she had vowed to stay out of his life. Perhaps she would even take her wayward daughter and return to the country.

He pushed away from the wall, the need for action gripping him. He simply couldn't allow that to happen. He must move quickly. What, he wondered, should he do?

The door opened behind him and more "guests" entered the smoky room. The female beside Sinclair gave up on him and wandered over to the latest arrivals.

"Wot can I get you t' drink, gents?"

"Nothing for me," said one of the newcomers gruffly.

"Brandy," growled the companion.

Lansdown slithered up to them, rubbing his hands. "What's your pleasure tonight, gentlemen? Cards, whiskey, or a bit of physical satisfaction?"

"We, uh, we just wanted to watch the game first."

Lansdown scowled, but he recovered and, poking the smaller man in the ribs, said, "Right you are, lad, but which game? The ladies or the cards?"

"Just the cards," said the young man, his voice squeaking nervously.

Neville moved a step closer, frowning slightly.

The hostess returned with the one glass and handed it to the smaller man. Linking her arms with theirs, she proceeded to promenade around the room with them.

"See anything that suits your fancy, gentlemen, you just tell Sadie. I'll make sure you receive full satisfaction, no matter what game you choose. And through that door, up the stairs, well, there's a cozy spot, secluded-like, for you and your chosen one. Here's Lucy; a sweet little thing, just up from the country, she is. She'd be happy to . . . Hey! What's the idea?"

"Never mind! Come along, you two! Sinclair, get the coats!"

"What th' deuce, Neville? I'm winning! I'm not leaving . . . Hey! Damn, cash me in. Wait a minute, Nev. Oh, devil take you! Well, where are the coats, man? Hurry up about it!" Sinclair hurried after the retreating trio. "Bloody hell, Neville, why the devil—"

"Shut up, Sinbad!"

"Really," growled the shorter of Neville's two prisoners.

"You shut up, too. Especially you," he added, frowning fiercely at the shorter of the two "gentlemen." He threw open the door of his carriage, and hustled them all inside.

Sinclair shut the door and sat down, grumbling under his breath, "Bloody cheek, I was winning, and he says—"

"Keep a civil tongue in your head, Sinbad," said Neville.

"I'm going to plant you a facer, Neville, if you tell me to shut up one more time! Who the deuce are these fellows, and why the—"

"These are not fellows, Sinbad." Reaching forward, Neville removed the hats of their two companions, his actions leaving Sinbad Sinclair, for once in his life, dumbfounded.

"You really are the most irritating man!"

"Oh, Phoebe, how can you say that?" wailed Charlotte, tears welling up in her brown eyes and spilling down her cheeks.

"Oh, I say . . ." murmured Sinbad, patting Charlotte's knee without thinking and fishing for his handkerchief.

Phoebe looked on with disgust. When she returned her attention to Sir Neville, he was shaking his head in amazement.

"You really have no feminine sensibilities, do you, Miss Fairfax?"

"Very few."

"Your mother will be appalled, you know. Why, only today, she promised me you would cause me no more trouble. I suppose I'm becoming gullible in my *old* age, but I actually believed her."

"It's not my fault you happen to be everywhere I go," said Phoebe, showing no sign of remorse.

"Tell me, do you never go anywhere acceptable? This is the third time I have discovered you in—I shall be kind and say unfortunate circumstances."

Phoebe had the grace to squirm uncomfortably, but she looked him in the eye and replied, "We were supposed to go to a rout and a ball tonight, but my mother decided we should stay home after she found out about that mare you bought for me."

"I see. Instead, you came to one of the worst examples of a gaming hell in all of London."

"I had no idea what it would be like," she pouted. "And I didn't intend to ruin your evening, especially not after you bought Flame for me."

"Flame? Oh yes, the mare. By the way, when were you going pay me for her?"

"I, uh, I can pay you part now, and part on the first of each month when I get my pin money."

"You know, gentlemen do not welch on debts of honor to other gentlemen. I don't wish to be disobliging, but you seem determined to make a study of the ways of gentlemen."

"I know. I'll ask my mother to advance . . ." She fell silent as he waved his hand languidly.

"Never mind, my dear. I make her a gift to you—in a fatherly way, of course."

"There's no need for that!"

"Oh, but I think there is. Taking money from an innocent is not quite proper. Now, brace yourselves; we are home."

"Oh, Phoebe!" wailed Charlotte.

"Here now, Miss . . . "

"Sweet," sobbed Charlotte.

"I'll just go in with you. I'm sure your parents will forgive you," said Sinbad.

Charlotte let out an even louder sob, shaking her head.

"I . . . I shall insist!" declared Sinbad Sinclair, who had never been in the petticoat line before, but would have lied to Saint Peter himself to calm down this distraught beauty.

"You are most kind, sir, but it would probably be best if we go in alone," said Phoebe, hopping down and dragging Charlotte after her.

Sinbad, who was suffering from Charlotte's tears almost as greatly as she was herself, took hold of her hand and declared himself ready to defend her against anyone. The scene threatened to turn into a tug of war with Charlotte as the rope, until Neville ended it by shoving Sinbad out of the carriage and following rapidly himself.

"There truly is no need, Sir Neville."

"On the contrary, Miss Fairfax. I would be much remiss in my, shall we say, fatherly duties, if I did not speak to your mother."

The door to the salon burst open, and all four members of that noisy carriage ride fell into the room. The sight of a calm Lady Annabelle quietly stitching a chair cover caused Charlotte to sob louder, Sinbad to expostulate volubly on her behalf, Phoebe to reiterate angrily that she did not need Sir Neville's escort, and Sir Neville to execute an elegant bow, his smile infuriating both Annabelle and her daughter.

"Phoebe, take Charlotte and go to your rooms. Sir Neville, pray be seated. And Mr. . . . ?"

"Sinclair, my lady, Sinbad Sinclair," said the younger man, bowing hastily.

"Mother! Don't listen to a word he has to say!"

"Phoebe, to your room!" said Annabelle, pointing the way. "And this time stay there!"

"I say, my lady, I really don't think Miss Sweet is in any condition to be punished. She is so very distraught."

"Mr. Sinclair, I assure you, Charlotte will be fine. She always gets that way when they have been found out. She will soon recover."

"Tell you what, Sinbad, why don't you take my carriage and go to the club. I'll see you there later," said Neville, shepherding his friend to the door.

When Neville turned back to her, Annabelle said

firmly, "You may as well join him, Sir Neville, as I have no intention of discussing my daughter with you."

"I can understand your chagrin," said Neville, ignoring her suggestion and taking the seat beside her on the sofa. "But I have begun to feel Miss Phoebe is in need of a stronger hand than you can give."

Annabelle's emerald eyes flashed with fire. "How thoughtful," she murmured. "But I can handle my daughter without your help."

"Can you? And what would you say if I told you Phoebe and Charlotte, dressed as young gentlemen once again, entered a rather infamous gaming establishment in Pall Mall." He was glad to see he had Annabelle's attention now. She grew pale as he continued, "On the arm of a 'lady' of dubious character, they were offered—as young men—to sample the entertainment there."

"Gambling," she breathed.

"And other more sensual amusements," he said quietly, marveling at her calm demeanor when he knew her emotions had to be reeling. "You do understand the gravity of the situation in which I found the young ladies, don't you?"

But Annabelle masked her horror and said coldly, "No doubt you will tell me since you were also present at this den of iniquity. While I do not condone my daughter's presence there, I feel quite strongly that if it is such a disreputable establishment, then you and Mr. Sinclair . . . Forgive me for my plain speaking, Sir Neville, but there is an expression about the pot calling the kettle black which seems to apply here."

"Surely you can't compare my actions to those of two innocent young ladies."

"Perhaps not, but they went there ignorant of the

debauchery they would find. You, on the other hand, were fully cognizant of the activities there, I believe.''

Sir Neville squirmed and said defensively, ''Perhaps you don't understand the danger they put themselves in. What if they had been discovered?''

Annabelle rose and extended her hand. ''While I thank you for your services to my daughter and her friend, Sir Neville, I believe I will be able to manage.''

Neville stood by her side, towering over her. He took her small hand in his and held it.

''What will you do?''

''That is none of your concern.''

''But it is,'' he said, raising her hand to his lips.

Annabelle did not jerk her hand away, but she trembled. Still, the lights in her green eyes were angry, and she waited silently for him to take his leave.

This will never do, thought Neville. If I leave now, she'll go back to the country on the morrow and then what will I do?

''I hope the young ladies were not recognized,'' he said.

''But they were. Not only by you, but by your friend, Mr. Sinclair.''

''You're not suggesting we will spread gossip,'' he said with a frown.

''I can only hope.''

''I had no idea you held such a low opinion of me,'' said Neville. Annabelle resisted the urge to reassure him, and he continued stiffly, ''But someone might find out about it, and you may need me to help squelch the rumors.''

''It is very kind of you to—''

''Surely you're not going back to the country,'' he said, alarmed. ''That would prove her guilt to the Ton!''

"I'm not certain what I shall do, but that is always a possibility."

"My dear Annabelle, perhaps I painted too harsh a picture. Phoebe and Charlotte were only having a bit of a lark."

Annabelle ignored his familiar use of her name and said sharply, "A lark? Sir Neville, I find your about-face very puzzling. On the one hand, you seem determined to paint the blackest picture possible; then you insist it was nothing but a lark. I think it a very good thing you never had children—or a wife; both would have stayed in a constant state of confusion. Now, I really must insist you leave me to my task. Thank you again."

There was nothing left for him to do but depart. Striding down the street, Neville congratulated himself heartily that he did not have a wife, or children, and was never likely to have either. He was delighted his nephew was such a capable manager of his estates so he had no qualms about securing another heir.

As for Lady Annabelle Fairfax, he hoped their paths never crossed again!

Chapter Five

During the course of the week that followed, Neville tried to convince himself he was over his unfortunate infatuation with Lady Annabelle Fairfax. He attended the play with Camilla and hardly looked twice toward the occupants of Lord Sweet's popular box. He couldn't help but feel Annabelle's presence, but he refrained from gazing at her like a lovesick puppy. He congratulated himself on his accomplishment, feeling this set him well on the road to recovery.

The next afternoon, he drove Camilla down Rotten Row at the fashionable hour and did not even strain his neck searching the crowd for Annabelle's auburn hair. He saw Phoebe riding in Lord West's carriage with her maid, two grooms dressed in Lord Sweet's livery following on horseback.

Later in the week, he attended a ball and somehow tamed the desire to dance with her. She was wearing a cream-colored gown with sparkling emeralds at her throat and on her wrists. Her beauty almost set him on his heels, and it required leaving almost as soon as he had arrived, but he won. Yes, he thought, congratulating himself; he was doing quite well without her.

It wasn't easy, certainly not with his friend extolling the virtues of Charlotte Sweet every time they met. As a matter of fact, Neville began avoiding Sinbad almost as arduously as he avoided Lady Annabelle. It was not a difficult task since Sinbad Sinclair neglected his friends at White's in favor of worshipping at Miss Sweet's feet.

By the following week, Sir Neville's routine consisted of rising early after late-night outings and taking long, solitary rides in the park. He spent hours in his attic studio trying to paint without turning out another attempt at capturing those captivating green eyes. All his efforts required a great deal of self-discipline and succeeding engendered a sense of pride in his self-control.

The fact that Sir Neville no longer made his almost daily trips to the Royal Academy to study the masters there merely served to create a more efficient household. Maltby's acerbic comments on his servants' predilection for laziness had, perforce, ceased. With Neville popping down from his studio at any hour of the day or night, they were in a constant state of readiness to display their dedication to serving him.

Maltby's concern for Sir Neville, however, grew daily. He had never known "the major" to act so strangely. But then, Maltby had never seen him in love. Oh, there had been the occasional ladybird like Lady Rand-Smythe, but Sir Neville's interests had been primarily physical.

This Lady Fairfax, though Maltby had never seen her in person, had been described in great detail to him by the butler. And it didn't require an overabundance of intelligence to know the major was well and truly caught.

When Maltby entered the studio late one afternoon, he discovered the major gazing at an unfinished canvas. The beauty captured on it had emerald eyes, and even old Maltby sighed in admiration.

"Lady Fairfax?" he asked.

"It was," said Sir Neville, coating a brush with blue paint. "But now it's going to be a landscape." With a violent blue stroke, he slashed across the beauty's forehead.

Maltby gasped, but he didn't dare protest. His eyes beneath those bushy brows were troubled, and Sir Neville took pity on the old man, favoring him with a weak smile.

Taking a rag and wiping away the blue paint, he said ruefully, "It wouldn't work anyway. I can't erase her from my mind."

On the tenth day of Sir Neville's self-imposed regimen of solitude, broken only by the occasional hand of cards at White's, Maltby decided to take matters into his own hands and bearded the lion in his den once again. He had debated whether it was his duty to interfere or if it was simply a desire to see the major happy again. Either way, he could no longer ignore the major's pain.

"Excuse me, sir," said the grizzled old batman, standing on the portal of Neville's attic studio.

"Yes, Maltby. What is it?"

"I have just heard the most extraordinary tale, major. I was wondering, sir, if you might know anything about it."

"If you're telling me Napoleon has escaped, or the old king has died, I might be interested. If, however, it's some inane bit of social gossip, I don't wish to hear it.''

Maltby tugged at the scraggly gray hairs covering his chin and debated on the possibility of retreat. But he plucked up his courage and said, '' 'Tis probably nothing, but there's t' be a duel in the morning.''

"Young idiots," muttered Neville, his brow knitting together.

"You are probably right, sir, but I did hear tell it was between two young ladies.''

"Probably just rubbish, Maltby. I'm surprised you listen to gossip—especially servants' gossip.''

"Aye, but that's where the real stories are," said the old man, nodding in satisfaction as he made his way back down the many flights of stairs.

Neville shrugged and returned to his painting. After a few more strokes, he slashed a huge green "X" through the still life and pitched his brush into the turpentine.

Ignoring Maltby's rumor was impossible; a duel was just the sort of "adventure" Phoebe might try. Neville had no way of knowing, of course, but he hoped he might discover Annabelle at the Royal Academy. He could have called at the Sweets' town house, but he had no desire to be rebuffed at the front door. He was greeted by one of the caretakers.

"Good afternoon, Sir Neville. Have you been out of town, sir? We haven't seen you in over a week."

"No, Roberts, I've been busy. Actually, I'm looking for a friend. Perhaps you can tell me if she is here.''

"Would that be Lady Rand-Smyth?" asked the man coyly.

"Who? No, it's a Lady Annabelle Fairfax.''

"Fairfax? A petite woman with auburn hair?"

"Yes, that is she," said Neville, carefully keeping his voice even. If he appeared too interested, Roberts, a notorious gossip, would no doubt mention it to anyone who happened to be visiting the Academy.

"No, sir, I haven't seen her in some time. Like you, it has been a week or ten days since the lady has come in. She's quite an artist, reminds me of you, she does, sitting for hours at one painting with her pastels. But no, she's not been . . ."

Neville didn't remain to hear more. He should have gone straight to see Annabelle instead of hanging back out of fear. Funny, he thought, in the army, no one ever questioned his courage, but a snip of a woman had him cowering in fear. Cursing himself for a fool, he drove straight to the Sweet town house only to be informed Lady Fairfax was not receiving.

As the door closed, he heard a giggle followed by a deeper laugh which sounded suspiciously like Sinbad Sinclair. Neville hurried down the steps and climbed into his curricle, his face like a thundercloud. Antonio clung to the back for dear life as the team jumped forward. Just as quickly, the team plunged to a halt.

"What the deuce?"

Neville watched with a frown as a groom astride a sorrel mare entered the street and turned toward Green Park. He watched for a moment, wondering at the heavy coat and hat pulled so far down; the groom must have had difficulty seeing. Then a smile formed on his lips, and at a sedate pace, Neville followed.

Inside the park, Neville shadowed the mare as far as he could in his equipage; then he jumped down, handing the ribbons to Antonio. Walking quickly, he followed on foot down a little-used, overgrown path, coming out into the open again at a small, ornamental pond. There, the mare cropped the abundant grass while the "groom" sat on the ground, arms hugging his drawn-up knees.

"On another adventure, Phoebe?"

The groom looked up, her eyes swimming with tears.

"Here now, what's all this about? Don't tell me your mother's disowned you or something," he teased, going to join her on the grass, wondering briefly if his buff-colored pantaloons would ever be the same.

"What do you care? You're part of the reason."

"I? May I ask how? I'm not even allowed inside your home."

"I don't see why not! After all, it was you who took us home in disgrace!"

"Ah, I'm sorry about that." At her sniff of disbelief, Neville said, "It has been a rotten Season all around. I never expected . . . Well, it hasn't turned out exactly as either of us planned, has it?" He handed her his handkerchief.

Phoebe stretched out her legs, blew her nose, and looked up at him thoughtfully.

"And what was your plan?" she asked.

"To have a jolly time this Season," he hedged.

"So was mine, and I was until . . ."

"Until I took you home from one of the worst gambling hells in London."

Phoebe perked up, giggling despite herself. "It was certainly dreadful," she agreed amicably. "But we came to no harm, you must admit."

"And you must admit, you don't know what would have happened if I hadn't stepped in."

She had the grace to acknowledge this and added dismally, "But now my mother is really keeping a close watch on us. We don't go anywhere without our maid and two footmen in attendance. It is so dreadful!"

"Such is the case with many young ladies, I think."

"Well, it wasn't that way before, not for me."

"Trust is always difficult to regain. Your mother only worries about you," said Neville, trying on this role of father. It made him feel positively ancient.

"My mother has entirely too much time on her hands! And as for Charlotte—she is no help whatsoever! Since she met that silly friend of yours, she doesn't have time for a lark! When she is not actually in his company, she is mooning about, sighing for him and writing the most dreadful poetry."

"Sinclair is courting Charlotte?" asked Neville, incredulous at the idea of his gambling, drinking, daredevil friend finding pleasure in such a tame activity. He knew he hadn't seen Sinclair at White's recently, but he hadn't considered the reason for his absence.

"Yes, he is always under foot," said Phoebe. "And my mother is delighted; she wants me to find someone just like him!"

"And you don't want to? I thought all girls came to London to do just that."

"Not I, and not Charlotte either until she met Sinclair. We wanted to have fun for another year or two before becoming someone's dull wife!"

Neville laughed out loud. "I cannot imagine your being a dull anything, Miss Phoebe."

She sniffed and said, "Thank you." Silence descended on them, but it was not awkward, each being caught up in his own thoughts of injustice.

Finally, Neville rose and stretched. "I would love to help you with your mother, but she is probably in the right. And what is more, I fear I have no influence with her anyway."

"Oh, I know. She detests you."

"Ah, I see," said Neville, his countenance falling and

his heart growing heavy. So much for his progress in forgetting about Annabelle.

Phoebe lifted her hands for him to pull her to her feet. When she was standing beside him, she cocked her head to one side and said, "You know, Sir Neville, you might be of some help to me."

Now is the time to run, thought Neville warily. Instead, he said, "How, may I ask?"

"Before all of this became so complicated, Charlotte and I had determined that the best thing we could do would be to provide my mother with someone else to occupy her time and thoughts."

"Someone else?" he echoed, throwing caution to the wind and thinking privately that *he* would be happy to be that "someone else."

"Yes, what Mother needs is a husband, preferably a widower with several children for her to look after." She misinterpreted his look of consternation and added hastily, "I know she's not very young, but she is still quite pretty, I think, and she could be a good wife to some older gentleman. She runs an efficient household, not to mention managing the estate."

Neville swallowed his agitation and said in strangled tones, "Did you have anyone in mind?"

"No. That's just the problem. Although I have met some older men, I can't very well inquire as to their fortune; people would get the wrong idea. But I certainly don't want Mother to fall into the hands of a fortune hunter. Although the estate will someday be mine, my mother has a comfortable competence of her own. Besides, the only older men Charlotte and I know are her father's political friends, and Mother would never settle for one of them."

"She wouldn't?" he said, the seed of an idea beginning to germinate.

"Certainly not. They are all town people. They almost never leave London, and all they ever talk about is the Whigs or Tories; they are dreadful bores. My mother is accustomed to country living. She runs our estate all by herself, sees to the needs of our tenants, and participates in all sort of church charity work," added Phoebe with pride. "So you see, she would make a wonderful wife for a countryman."

"Perhaps there is someone at home . . ."

"No, no one. There is the vicar, but he is much too stuffy, and Mother will not tolerate someone telling her what to do and how to do it. She has been her own mistress for so long, you see."

"No, I didn't know. I knew she was a widow, but I—"

"Yes, my father died three months before I was born. My mother is quite independent, as you can imagine."

A smile spread across Neville's handsome face; the corners of his eyes crinkled in amusement. Phoebe watched him expectantly.

"I really haven't thought about the men I know as being husband material or not, you understand."

"Of course not," she replied.

"But if you were to point out the ones you think might be appropriate for her, I could make inquiries, very discreet inquiries, as to their fortunes and suitability."

"Would you truly do that for me?"

He swept an elegant bow, saying, "It would be a privilege, Miss Phoebe." Seeing she was not convinced, he added, "It's the honorable thing for me to do, I suppose, since my actions have led to your virtual incarceration. There is one more issue I must ask you about first, however."

"And that would be?"

"You haven't any plans to duel at sunup tomorrow morning, have you?"

She laughed and shook her head, sending her red curls bouncing.

"Good," he said. "Then we have an understanding?"

Phoebe favored him with a sunny smile and extended her hand. With a firm handshake, they sealed their bargain.

Chapter Six

Annabelle had no idea what had caused the change in Phoebe from the day before, but she was thankful for it all the same. Just as suddenly as Phoebe had become silent and taciturn, she had returned to her usual cheerful self. And as she did, Annabelle's distrust began to fall away. The strain between them was so unusual, it had robbed Annabelle of her peace of mind. That, alongside her preoccupation with Sir Neville Colston, had caused her many sleepless nights.

Now, all that was at an end. Phoebe had come down to breakfast that morning a changed person. She had chattered on about the ball they were to attend that night, and now, gazing across Lady Goforth's ballroom, Annabelle watched her beautiful daughter charm her elderly partner.

"Your daughter is certainly being an accommodating child this evening, my dear Annabelle," said her hostess, appearing at her elbow. "After I saw her dancing with old General Smithfield, I congratulated her on being so kind to him, and she told me she likes nothing better than the intelligent conversation of older men.''

Annabelle's eyes narrowed at such a blatant exaggeration, but she only smiled and said, "She's a sweet girl."

"I fear, however, she may be neglecting her younger beaux. I overheard Lord West, whom I know is one of her particular friends, complaining to his friend Mr. Good that he despaired of signing her card for a single dance. Truly, kindness is a wonderful trait, but a young lady must always be thinking about marriage. She wouldn't want to discourage her suitors. I hate to interfere, but I thought it best to drop a hint, you know— since you are not exactly in your element here in London."

"Thank you so much, Agnes," said Annabelle haughtily. Really, the woman had not changed one whit since their days together at Miss Brown's Seminary for Young Ladies. The daughter of a marquis, she had always felt it her "duty" to help those on a lower social level.

When the promenade that ended the quadrille brought Phoebe within hailing distance, Annabelle called her daughter to her.

Quickly, before the young men could assail her, she whispered, "Why is it you are disappointing all your young beaux, Phoebe? You mustn't play too hard to get."

"I'm not, Mother. I have saved several dances for them, but I have yet to speak to them. I did tell Lord West I had saved the supper dance for him."

"That's better, then," said Annabelle. "You seem to be enjoying yourself."

"I am. But Mother, why don't you dance? With Lady Margaret still away, you must be bored beyond belief sitting with the chaperons."

"It is kind of you to be concerned about me, Phoebe,

but I am quite content; don't worry about me. Now, here is Mr. Waverly. Good evening, sir."

The evening slipped past. Annabelle remained with the other chaperons and mothers, lending only half an ear to the incessant gossip. She hated to admit that Phoebe was right, but she was bored without her friend. Margaret had written that it might be several more days before she could return; the thought of many more evenings spent in agonizing boredom was almost unbearable.

Annabelle smoothed her royal blue gown and played with the strings of her reticule. Smiling and nodding occasionally, she vowed to survive the night. She almost hoped Phoebe would do something outrageous so she would have the excuse of dragging her away early.

Phoebe, she thought, her eyes raking the ballroom. There was Charlotte, talking to her friend Goodie with a frowning Mr. Sinclair by her side. Annabelle almost giggled; Mr. Sinclair's boyish face and golden hair made him look like a disgruntled cherub.

Returning to her original quarry, she stood up and scanned the assembly. Phoebe was nowhere to be seen. Probably in the ladies' retiring room. Annabelle excused herself and began to search quietly for her daughter.

"*Shh,*" whispered Phoebe, tugging urgently at Sir Neville's sleeve, pulling him farther into Lady Goforth's darkened garden. "Do you want someone to recognize us?"

When they were in a secluded area, Neville said, "No, young minx, the last thing I want is to be accused of compromising you!"

She laughed, taking no offense at his words. "No more than I!" she exclaimed.

"I see you have been busy tonight. Have you picked out a husband for your mother?"

She nodded, saying, "I have danced with and been stepped on by more elderly men tonight than ever in my whole life. Is there some rule that makes old men forget how to dance? My feet will be black and blue tomorrow!"

"Sacrifice has its price," he said dryly. "But tell me who the candidates are."

"First, there is Lord Blackstone; he is not too very old. Perhaps your age."

Neville frowned but refrained from telling her that Blackstone was at least sixty to his seven and thirty. Instead, he said, "A little too long in the tooth, I think. His spinster daughter is older than your mother and still lives at home with him. Not, I think you'll agree, a pleasant situation to wish upon your mother."

"Hmm, I suppose not. What about Mr. Prufrock? He is rather handsome, I suppose."

"Prufrock? That pompous bore? You must be kidding! Phoebe, I thought you cared for your mother. Really, you must try harder than that! Prufrock! Pah!"

"You needn't be rude," she snapped. "I've only just begun. Why don't you think of someone? You must know everyone in London; you have lived here for years, I understand."

"Since the war."

"Right! Three years is a long time! And you could ask Mr. Sinclair to help."

"Sinbad? He's completely useless since he's head over heels about your friend. Hasn't even been to the club in the past week!"

"Really? You know, this love thing is really rather

frightening. I'm quite relieved my mother is past that sort of thing."

"Being much too old, of course," drawled Neville.

"Well, yes. I mean, I am not so naive to think Mother has one foot in the grave, but she is past such romantic notions! What she needs is a comfortable companion—someone she can take care of after I have married in a year or two."

"You are really quite selfless," he observed dryly.

"Thank you," said Phoebe, frowning as she reviewed the partners she had endured. "What about Mr. Duncan? He wasn't too pompous. And he's not that old, I don't think."

"Duncan? I don't know him, really. I'll make some inquiries," said Neville, wondering what objection he could make to this man who was possessed of a fortune, was kind to his elderly mother, helped orphans, and was only forty years old.

"Perhaps we could meet tomorrow morning by the pond."

"Perhaps," said Neville. "For now, we should get back before we are missed. You go first; I'll follow after a decent interval."

"Thank you, Sir Neville."

"My pleasure, Miss Fairfax," he said, smiling at her retreating figure. What a minx! And was he really aspiring to matrimony with her mother?

The thought gave Neville pause, and he turned the idea over and over in his mind. Yes, he supposed he really was contemplating marriage with Annabelle. Contemplating? He was bloody-well desperate with determination. Never mind that she couldn't bear the sight of him at the moment. He would win her; he had to. He couldn't imagine life going on as it had before they met, and knew now he didn't want to imagine life without her.

When Neville returned to the ball, his gaze traveled immediately to the group of matrons where he had last seen Annabelle. She wasn't there, and it took him a few minutes to locate her moving from one knot of people to another. He saw her relax and smile slightly as she spotted Phoebe. She must have remarked upon her daughter's absence from the ballroom. Thank heavens he and Phoebe had concluded their "business" before Annabelle had searched in the gardens! Neville shivered at the thought of being forced to wed the daughter of the woman he planned to marry. It rather sounded like a farce he had seen recently at the theater. A nightmare more like! he thought.

Annabelle returned to the matrons, and Neville continued to watch her whenever she wasn't looking in his direction.

For her part, Annabelle struggled never to look in Sir Neville Colston's direction. Wasn't it enough that his gray eyes and dark good looks invaded her sleep? And when she was alone, stitching on that boring chair cover, he inevitably popped into her thoughts without warning. Never mind that she had given up going to the Royal Academy after narrowly missing running into him the day after Sir Neville had saved Phoebe and Charlotte from the gaming hell! Whenever she picked up her watercolors or pastels, his face came to mind, teasing her and making her completely miserable. The man was odiously intrusive!

"Good evening, Lady Fairfax."

"Good evening, Mr. Duncan."

"I was wondering if I might have the next dance, my lady?"

Taken by surprise, Annabelle accepted. Mr. Duncan

took her in his arms at precisely the prescribed distance and waltzed her onto the dance floor. Neville pushed away from the pillar he was holding up and glared at the couple fiercely.

Annabelle looked up at her attractive partner and smiled. He was not so tall as "you-know-who," she told herself, but he was a very competent dancer. And his embrace didn't cause her the same torment which Sir Neville's had. As a matter of fact, she thought, she felt quite comfortable in Mr. Duncan's arms.

"Do you live in London all year long, Mr. Duncan?" she asked, lifting her face to his.

"No, my estate is near Oxford. My mother lives with me, but she wanted to come to London for a few weeks during the Season, and I felt obliged to accompany her."

"How kind of you," said Annabelle.

"I understand you live in Berkshire, my lady."

"Yes, we have an estate there."

"And you manage it yourself?" he asked. Annabelle nodded, and he said gallantly, "Then we are especially fortunate you were able to get away at this busy time of the year."

"Thank you, sir. But you must know, I am presenting my daughter Phoebe this Season."

"As a matter of fact, I did know. I danced with that young lady earlier."

Annabelle wondered if this waltz was perhaps a way for him to get to know Phoebe better. Really, Mr. Duncan was a charming man, but much too old for Phoebe. She had better set about discouraging him.

"Yes, Phoebe is quite a handful. She's a charmer, to be sure, but she will get into scrapes. She is most accustomed to life in the country, and chafes at the restrictions placed upon her as a young lady of Ton."

"Oh, of course. But you shall soon be rid . . . That is, she will no doubt find a husband this Season, and then you may be comfortable again."

"I assure you, Mr. Duncan, having my daughter with me does *not* make me uncomfortable. She is the light of my life."

"Certainly, I meant no offense, my lady. I . . . but here is the end of our delightful dance. Thank you."

"My pleasure," she said stiffly.

Annabelle found herself standing with fists clinched and lips pursed. Really, the arrogance of the man! Why, he was no better than . . .

"Good evening, Lady Fairfax," said Neville, causing her to jump. "Sorry if I startled you. I was going to request a dance, but I see it is the boulanger—not a favorite of mine. Perhaps you'd like some champagne, or a breath of fresh air."

Indeed, Annabelle thought she was being strangled by her emotions—first Duncan's impertinence and now Sir Neville. Without thinking, Annabelle nodded, not knowing or caring if she was agreeing to champagne or fresh air. In the end, she received both; Neville swept two glasses off the tray of a passing servant as he ushered her out the French doors and onto the large stone terrace. He waited in silence as she gulped down the bubbly liquid and cleared her throat with a cough.

Neville found it difficult to be so close and not have the license to, at the very least, put his arm around her waist. Trying for a light topic, Neville looked beyond the dense gardens to the sloping lawns that led to the gently flowing Thames.

"I think if I were to make London my home permanently, I would buy a place like this, outside the city, away from all the noise and crowds."

"It is nice here," said Annabelle, coming to her senses

and realizing with dismay that she had obligated herself to spend the duration of this dance with the one man who haunted her every waking and sleeping thought.

"Is Miss Phoebe enjoying herself this evening? I've never seen her in better looks."

"Yes, I think she is."

"No more adventures?"

Annabelle's features hardened, and Neville wished he had bitten his tongue.

"When I think of her," he said, playing for time as he tried to extricate himself from his *faux pas*, "I visualize a wood nymph, a little sprite. She is so curious and lively; she'll be quite a catch for some lucky young man."

Annabelle stepped away from him and searched the angular planes of his face before she granted him a slight smile. Here, she thought, was someone who appreciated Phoebe for what she was and didn't try to make her fit the tight little mold the Ton found acceptable.

"Thank you," she said quietly.

"You're welcome."

"There are times I find it almost overwhelming, the decisions thrust upon me as a mother."

Her smile was a plea for understanding, and Neville said sincerely, "Phoebe's a lovely child, high-spirited, to be sure, but you would not want a milk and water miss."

"No, I would not," said Annabelle with a grateful smile.

Silence descended on them, the strains of the music fading away in the serenity of the moonlight. Annabelle's gloved hands held the stone railing, and Neville moved his hand slightly to touch hers. The moon disappeared behind a cloud, leaving them in deep shadows. Neville's hand covered hers; his fingers caught hers up, and he lifted her hand to his chest. Turning to face her, he stepped closer, capturing her other hand and lifting both to his lips.

He bent his head, his strong arms encircled her waist, bringing her closer. Annabelle closed her eyes as their lips met in a kiss so gentle, she would later wonder if she had only imagined it.

"Annabelle, I . . ."

Giggles erupted from the house, and footsteps tripped across the terrace and down the steps.

"La, West, you are a rogue! I warrant you'll land me in the suds again!"

"Phoebe," whispered Annabelle, her attention ripped from Neville instantly.

Frustrated anger settled on Neville's shoulders like a demon, and he strode across the terrace and down the steps in Phoebe's wake. Annabelle remained frozen on the upper level, peering through the darkness to no avail.

The path was lighted only by moonlight, and Neville stopped, no longer guided by Phoebe's giggling. Then it started again, and he sped forward.

"Come on, Phoebe, hold tight."

"I'm trying, but I'm slipping. I can't hold . . . Oh!"

"I've got you; I've got you. Try again. I'll boost you up. Put your arms around my neck."

"The devil, you say!" hissed Neville, grabbing hold of Lord West's collar and pulling him off balance.

A loud, long *"Ooooooh!"* was followed by a heavy thud as Phoebe fell to the ground.

"Phoebe!" exclaimed both men, West reaching out to touch her shoulder.

Neville's fist made contact with the other speaker's mouth, and West dropped to the ground beside Phoebe.

"Get on your feet, you scoundrel!" growled Neville.

Phoebe scrambled to her feet and grabbed Neville's hands. "Stop this! Stop this immediately! What in the world are you doing, Sir Neville? Leave him alone!"

Neville focused on her and said tersely, "Stay out of this, Phoebe. Return to your mother at once!"

"I will not! You are not my father, and I'll not do as you say! West was only trying to help me climb the observer's pole so I might see if Charlotte and Sinclair were in the maze."

"Observer's pole?"

"Yes. See?"

Neville's anger melted as he looked up, seeing the pole with its rungs beginning at eye level.

"Oh, I . . ." But what could he say? Taking refuge in righteous indignation, he said gruffly, "Phoebe, you shouldn't be out here without a chaperon. You have no idea—"

"I am not your daughter."

"Thank heavens for that!" he intoned, looking heavenward. Then he stretched out his hand and pulled the dazed and bewildered Lord West to his feet, brushing him off and clapping him on the back with a brief word of apology. He added quietly, "A bit of advice from an experienced bachelor: You must think twice before strolling in a dark garden with a young lady. You may find yourself saddled with her for life."

"Well!" said Phoebe, turning and marching back toward the light. Dazed, Lord West stumbled after her.

When Neville reached the terrace, he found it deserted. He entered the ballroom just in time to see Annabelle shepherding her daughter up the stairs to the ladies' withdrawing room.

"Blast!" he muttered, turning sharply as a curvaceous figure moved quickly to his side.

"Neville, my love, where have you been? Your cravat is

all askew, and you've a smudge on your cheek," gushed Camilla, taking a scrap of lace from her reticule and rubbing at the offensive mark.

Neville brushed her hand away, his eyes willing Annabelle to stop and look at him before she disappeared. As if she had heard his thoughts, Annabelle turned, searching the crowded ballroom for his face. She smiled; then she saw Camilla reach up possessively and straighten his cravat. The openness in Annabelle's eyes snapped closed, and she spun away.

"I haven't seen you since we went driving last week. Have you been out of town?" cooed Camilla.

"Camilla, please stop fussing with my cravat. I can straighten it myself. What's more, I'm leaving so it doesn't matter if it has come undone."

She ignored the irritation in his voice and asked sweetly, "Might I beg a ride back to town? I came with the Browns, and I'm afraid they've already left."

"Oh, very well. Send for your cloak."

"Cloak? Why, I am never cold. I have only this shawl so I shan't detain you at all, dear Neville."

She linked arms with him and held tightly as they left the ball.

In his carriage, Neville made no attempt to be civil, his thoughts still on Annabelle and their interrupted kiss on the terrace. What must she think of him now? he wondered. He wasn't certain he knew what to think either. Previously Annabelle had shown little sign of caring for him, but she had allowed him to kiss her.

Neville shook his head. "Does she allow just any man to kiss her?"

"Certainly not," purred Camilla, snuggling so close, she was practically sitting in his lap. "You are the only gentleman granted that privilege since my dear husband departed. You know that, Neville. I had begun to think

you didn't care anymore, but I can see I was wrong."
She lifted her gloved hand to caress his cheek.

Neville removed her hand, frowning down at her in
the gloom of the carriage.

"Camilla, I was not speaking of you. As a matter of
fact, until you responded, I was not aware that I had
spoken aloud at all. I had forgotten you were even in
the carriage."

With a toss of her head, she moved as far away as the
seat would allow.

"Don't tell me you've fallen for that Fairfax creature!
Why, you'll be the laughing stock of all the Ton!"

"Camilla, I warn you . . ."

"She says she came to London to find a husband for
that hoydenish daughter of hers, but it is obvious to
anyone of sense that she is fortune hunting for herself!"

"Camilla!"

"She has probably gone through the money her late
husband left her, and now she needs to marry someone
who can keep her in luxury and provide a large dowry
so she can buy a husband for her daughter!"

Neville shouted, "Stop the horses!" Reaching past
his passenger, he opened the door. "If you do not close
your venomous mouth this instant, Camilla, I shall throw
you out of this carriage here and now."

"You wouldn't dare!"

The clouds parted, showing plainly Neville's expression of anger and aversion. Camilla shivered and
nodded.

Snapping the door closed, Neville called to his driver,
"Spring 'em."

Neville awoke in a cold sweat, his heart pounding and
fists clenched. He climbed out of bed and staggered to

the table where a full decanter of Madeira rested. Pouring a full measure, he downed it quickly, gasping as it burned his throat.

He poured another glass. It warded off the early morning chill, but he stirred the fire anyway before settling into the dilapidated old chair he wouldn't allow anyone to throw out.

He placed the glass on the table by his side and ran his fingers through his hair.

It was bad enough when his dreams of Annabelle had disturbed his sleep with their provocativeness. This was ten times worse! Annabelle, taunting and teasing, gyrating seductively, but not for him! Instead, there had been Prufrock and Blackstone and that disgustingly eligible Duncan! What was she thinking? he asked himself before remembering it had only been a dream—his dream.

He reminded himself brutally that Annabelle was not his; he had never declared himself to her and wasn't certain she would have him, even if he did. She certainly hadn't shown him any partiality—quite the opposite, he admitted dismally.

"Maybe you should just do as you promised Phoebe and help her find a husband for Annabelle," he told the trembling flames. With an angry exclamation, he swallowed the remainder of the wine and threw the glass into the fire.

Annabelle thrust the covers away and swung her feet over the side of the bed. She walked to the dressing table and sat down before it, picking up the brush and running it through her tangled hair. How she had managed to unplait the tightly woven braid, she couldn't guess. She usually slept so soundly—so calmly.

Chapter Seven

Annabelle rose late the next morning, just in time to accompany the girls on their excursion to the Pantheon Bazaar. They were unusually silent, allowing her to withdraw further into herself. Annabelle, too wrapped up in her own thoughts, failed to discern the distance between the duo. As they descended from the carriage, Annabelle was startled out of her reverie upon hearing her name called.

"Lady Fairfax! Oh, Lady Fairfax!"

Annabelle turned to see Sinbad Sinclair hurrying toward them and smiled in greeting.

"Good afternoon, Mr. Sinclair," she said, extending her hand.

"Good afternoon, ladies. Now I know good fortune is smiling on me today," said Sinclair, his eyes lingering on Charlotte.

"What a surprise," drawled Phoebe, her tone causing Sinclair to blush and Charlotte to pinch her elbow.

Annabelle studied the young people, one brow rising

slightly. Charlotte turned away, pretending a great interest in a ribbon vendor's displays.

"Yes," said Annabelle, with a sharp look at her daughter, "a pleasant surprise. I know many gentlemen are bored by an afternoon spent in the shops, but would you care to join us, Mr. Sinclair?"

"If I might be of service to you ladies, I would be delighted."

With this invitation, Mr. Sinclair fell happily in line with the ladies, his hand touching Charlotte's arm frequently as they proceeded. He was patience personified as he followed the ladies through mountains of lace and trimmings, buttons and bonnets, carrying parcels, and when asked, carting them back to the carriage where the groom lounged happily.

"Is there anything else you need, girls?" asked Annabelle after two hours.

"I believe we have completed our errands," said Phoebe, poking the dreamy-eyed Charlotte in the ribs to remind her of her surroundings.

"Oh, I'm finished, too."

"Then perhaps you ladies might consent to honor me with your presence for some tea and ices at Gunter's?" asked Sinclair.

"How kind," said Annabelle. "Yes, we would love to join you."

The short journey to the famous tea room accomplished, Sinclair ushered the ladies inside, seeing to their every need. Even Phoebe was persuaded out her sullens by his glib tales of daring at the card table.

"I must say, Mr. Sinclair, I have never had a gentleman entertain me so thoroughly by relating the details of gaming and wagers," admitted Phoebe.

His face became flushed, and he turned to Annabelle, stammering, "I do hope, my lady, my stories were not inappropriate to tell the young ladies! I wouldn't dream of offering them insult!''

"And none was taken!" cried Charlotte.

Annabelle hurried to allay his uneasiness. "You may be easy on that point, Mr. Sinclair. There was nothing inappropriate, either in the telling or the facts. And while some men relating their prowess at the tables would make them appear egotistical, such is not the case with you."

Sinbad smiled and replied easily, "Perhaps that is because I am so very bad at gaming, my lady. Were I as lucky and skilled as Neville, then I might become a dead bore on the subject."

"Sir Neville is a gambler?" asked Phoebe.

"I'm not certain one can call him such since he inevitably wins. He has the devil's own luck at the tables. Oh, begging your pardon, ladies, I'm sure."

"No need, Mr. Sinclair. Girls, we really must be going. Your mother will be home shortly, Charlotte, and you will naturally want to be there to greet her," said Annabelle.

"Yes, yes, of course," said the dark-haired beauty, her heart in her eyes as she gazed at Mr. Sinclair.

"Come along, Charlotte," said Phoebe, pushing her friend before her as they made their way to the carriage.

"Lady Fairfax," said Sinclair, hanging back. "A word with you, if I may."

"Certainly, sir."

"You are the best of friends with Charlotte's—that is, Miss Sweet's parents." He ran a finger around the intricately tied cravat constricting his neck before continuing. "Do you think . . . that is, are you of the opinion . . ."

"Do I think they would approve?" said Annabelle, swallowing her amusement.

"Yes, I mean, I am not wealthy. I would say I am only comfortable, you see."

"How old are you, Mr. Sinclair?"

"I shall be thirty next month."

"A perfect age, I should think, for an eligible bachelor to go courting," said Annabelle, her smile telling him all he needed to know.

"Oh, thank you, my lady, thank you!"

"So I have decided to speak to her father tomorrow morning," said Sinbad, striding down the length of Neville's drawing room and back again.

"An admirable plan," agreed Neville, cutting another slice of the pear he was eating. Clad in a dressing gown of colorful brocade, he lounged on the striped sofa, his slippered feet propped up on the arm. "Do you plan to have a long engagement?"

"Engagement?" asked Sinbad, stopping in his tracks.

"Well, I mean, you can't very well ask for her hand one day and wed the next. There has to be some sort of engagement, or people will talk, and since Lord Sweet is politically minded, the last thing he would want is talk about his daughter."

"Yes, I see. Well, then I suppose there must be an engagement of at least a month or two. But I must say, Nev, I think it grossly unfair to get a fellow all fitted up for the parson's mousetrap, and then force him to stew about it for weeks on end!"

Neville laughed. Stretching his long legs, he sauntered to the sideboard to pour fresh drinks.

"Here's to you, Sinbad, and the lovely Miss Sweet."

* * *

"I cannot believe you are ready to go out tonight, Margaret, after riding in a closed carriage all day," said Annabelle, sitting at her dressing table and putting the finishing touches on her hair.

"If you had spent the past fortnight holding hands, mopping feverish brows, and soothing nonsensical fears and tears, you would understand completely!" exclaimed Margaret. She smiled knowingly at her friend's image and said, "Besides, I wouldn't want to deprive you of your evening of pleasure."

"I have no idea what you are talking about," said Annabelle, her mind flying to Sir Neville. She knew her face was flaming, but she tried to brave it out and met her friend's coy gaze coolly.

"Really? *Someone* informed me that you have been as much in demand at the balls as our girls have been. Indeed, someone told me Mr. Duncan couldn't quit talking about how light you are on your feet. And then there was—"

"Really, Margaret, your *someone* should mind his or her own affairs. I do not intend to stoop so low as to refute idle gossip."

With a girlish giggle, Margaret leaned down to see her own hair in the mirror and said, "I simply must have Mr. Vincent cut my hair tomorrow. I look positively savage!"

"You look wonderful, and you know it," said Annabelle, rising and putting her arm around her friend's waist to give her a quick hug. "And I think you may have other things to do on the morrow."

"Oh? What sort of things?"

"I shouldn't spoil the surprise, but sometimes it is best to be prepared. Your Charlotte has a young man."

"No! Really? Why, she never mentioned a word in her letters! Who is he? Perhaps Mr. Andrews?"

"No, no, not him. Really, Margaret, he is much too serious for Charlotte. No, this is a friend of Sir Neville Colston, a Mr. Sinclair."

"Sir Neville Colston? I can't see that being a friend of his is any recommendation. He is always seen with that Rand-Smythe creature. She is nothing but a hanger-on, as far as I'm concerned. And there he is, wasting his time on her when he has not only a prosperous estate in the country but a fortune in investments."

Annabelle struggled to set aside the churning emotions Margaret's comments had produced, and said, "Be that as it may, Mr. Sinclair is a charming young man who has been devoted to Charlotte since first he set eyes on her. You must give him the benefit of the doubt."

"I shall make inquiries," said Margaret. Then she added petulantly, "You would think the least that girl could reasonably do is fall in love with one of her father's political cronies."

"I believe where love is concerned, rationalism has little or no place."

"Then it is a good thing a girl is guided by rational parents," said Margaret as they descended the stairs.

Annabelle shook her head, no longer certain she had been correct in her assessment of the situation when she spoke to Mr. Sinclair. She watched as Charlotte came tripping down the stairs, stars in her eyes. Phoebe followed more sedately, a slight frown marring her forehead.

Annabelle pulled her aside and asked, "What is the matter, my dear?"

Phoebe huffed indignantly and nodded at Charlotte, saying, "She is being such a ninnyhammer, Mother. I may not be able to bear it much longer; I shall be forced to say something scathing about her foolishness."

Annabelle cautioned, "I know you have been less than pleased with Charlotte since Mr. Sinclair appeared."

"Well, she is such a ninny about the man," said Phoebe, allowing her disgust free rein again.

"That, my dear, is how people in love are supposed to act. But I must warn you, beg you, do not desert Charlotte now. Be patient with her; it may be that things will not go as she hopes." Annabelle nodded toward Lady Margaret. "She may need all your understanding very soon."

"Oh, Mother, I hope you may be wrong. I couldn't bear her being hurt."

"So do I, my love; so do I."

The evening began with a rout at Lord Hampton's. The ladies spent three-quarters of an hour fighting their way to the drawing room on the first floor just to greet their host. On the way down, Mr. Duncan met them, and instead of continuing his ascent, he followed them as they spent the same amount of time descending to street level and into their carriage to complete the short drive to Mr. and Mrs. Robertson's ball.

"So good of you to take me up," said Duncan, smiling at each lady in turn.

"Think nothing of it, sir. We are always happy to oblige a gentleman such as yourself," said Lady Margaret, glancing coyly at her friend.

Phoebe, too, smiled benignly on Mr. Duncan.

When they had made it through the receiving line at the Robertsons', Mr. Duncan requested the first waltz with Annabelle. She accepted, all the while looking over his shoulder for the familiar black and silver hair, the piercing gray eyes.

He isn't here, she concluded. All for the best, she

told herself, but could not deny the evening had suddenly fallen flat for her. She was dangerously close to losing her heart to the cynical Sir Neville, but she was not in the same class as he was. He not only enjoyed flirting, he was obviously very good at it. And until her journey to London, she had never indulged in even a mild flirtation.

Phoebe accepted the arm of Lord West and disappeared into the sea of faces. Lady Margaret surveyed the company, her expression growing increasingly haughty as Charlotte remained by her side, none of the young men approaching her.

"What is this?" she demanded of her daughter. "Have you managed to discourage all of them?"

"No, Mama, I—"

"Here is Mr. Good, Charlotte, come to beg a dance of you," said Annabelle hastily.

He made an elegant bow, doing the pretty with ease, and led Charlotte away.

"I don't understand it," grumbled Margaret. "I was only away a fortnight, and she has managed to alienate half the male populace of London by wearing her heart on her sleeve."

"Charlotte cannot help it if . . . she is not as skilled at hiding her feelings as . . ." Annabelle couldn't finish, aware that her own heart's desire was muddled at the moment and afraid of revealing this bewildering state of affairs to her perceptive friend.

She needn't have worried; Lady Margaret was much too preoccupied with her daughter to notice Annabelle's existence.

Her eyes narrowed, and Margaret said, "Well, I have returned now, and things will soon be back as they should be." She sailed away, joining a tight-knit group of matrons whose principal function in the Ton was the accumulation, and more importantly, the dissemination of gossip.

Annabelle shrugged and wandered toward another group of chaperons, whose gowns and demeanors proclaimed them to be paid companions or indigenous females who had managed to prove their usefulness in the households of their more fortunate relatives. Here, there were no jealous mamas, and the conversation was less viperish.

Dressed in a lavender silk gown with the fashionable high waist and low décolletage, Annabelle felt she blended in. Most of the ladies in this group wore modest grays and lavenders, but this small sea of unassuming females served only as a foil to Annabelle's beauty.

Neville saw her on the instant when he entered the ballroom. Her pale skin shone like iridescent opals among gray stone. The soft purple of her gown made her green eyes sparkle like emeralds.

He grinned at his own poetic thoughts, acknowledging that such drivel would at one time have sickened him, but he couldn't tear his eyes away from her.

"What the deuce? She's dancing with that Good fellow!" exclaimed Sinclair at Neville's elbow.

"No, she's not," replied Neville before realizing his friend was speaking about Charlotte Sweet and not his Annabelle. Reasonably, he added, "she had to dance with someone since you weren't here yet, and the fellow is only a friend, I believe."

Sinclair growled some response and shuffled away.

My Annabelle. Neville tried out the phrase; it brought a smile to his face.

There was a wave of movement as the music stopped. Neville elbowed a path through the press of people, slowly making his way to Annabelle's side. When he reached the group of wide-eyed chaperons, she was gone. The musicians launched into a waltz, and he turned, drawn to her like a moth to a flame.

"Duncan," he hissed.

"Good evening, Sir Neville," said another familiar voice at his side.

Reluctantly, Neville turned and greeted Phoebe.

"They really do make a nice couple, don't they?"

"Humph!"

"Would you like to get some refreshments with me, Sir Neville?" asked Phoebe, guiding him away from the interested gazes of the chaperons. When they had attained the relative quiet of the dining room, and she had handed him a glass of champagne, she said, "What about Duncan? Is he as suitable as he seems?"

Neville had always believed in telling the truth. Indeed, he had been known for it, had been asked upon numerous instances to serve as judge and jury over some wager. But as he looked down at Annabelle's daughter, he shook his head ruefully.

"I am sorry to tell you, Phoebe, but the man's a rogue and a rake. I can't reveal what I've learned, not to a young lady, but suffice it to say, he will not do for a decent lady like your mother."

"Really? What has he done? Do tell!" urged Phoebe, her eyes wide with curiosity.

"Oh, I couldn't, shouldn't say anything more, not to such an innocent young lady."

"Ooh," she breathed, her imagination supplying mysterious, unspeakable rituals. "Then we must look further. Oh my, she must be warned! Even now she is dancing with the scoundrel! And he rode beside her in the carriage! What shall we do?"

"What was the man doing in your carriage?" said Neville, unable to keep the hostility from his tone. At her quizzical stare, he continued more calmly, "Don't worry. I'll take care of Duncan; he shan't be leaving with you.''

"Oh, thank you, Sir Neville.''

"Good evening, Sir Neville.'' said Lord West, his hand instinctively rubbing his bruised jaw. "Phoebe, that is, Miss Fairfax, I was wondering where you had disappeared. There's to be a second waltz, and I have secured permission from Lady Drummond for you to join in.'' He looked cautiously at Neville, asking permission with his eyes. Sir Neville nodded imperceptibly.

"Really? Oh, West, you are the very best of friends!'' She kissed her fingertips to Neville and hurried away.

Neville left the quiet of the dining room and sauntered back to watch the end of the first waltz.

His eyes immediately sought out Annabelle. She is so graceful, thought Neville, admiring the way she glided around the floor. And I must admit, Duncan is holding Annabelle just as he ought. I may be forced to kill him, he thought, his right hand reaching instinctively for the sword he had once worn.

As the dancers promenaded before the next set, Neville swooped down on Duncan and Annabelle. Taking her free arm, he continued to circle with them, much to the chagrin of Duncan and the amusement of Annabelle.

The man is outrageous, she thought, carefully keeping her expression nonpartisan. She glanced at him out of the corner of her eye. He was wearing a black coat and pantaloons with a silver waistcoat. His cravat was simply tied, and a diamond glittered in its folds. He was several inches taller than Mr. Duncan, and his waist was as trim as a man of twenty.

Neville stopped, bringing Annabelle and, perforce, Duncan to a halt as well. "That's it, old chap. Time for you to go, Duncan. My turn now,'' he said cheerfully.

Ignoring Neville, Mr. Duncan bowed over Annabelle's hand and thanked her for the pleasure of her company, but Neville was already leading her away from him.

"Good, I'm glad he's gone," said Neville, taking her hand in his.

"You didn't ask if I were free for this set," she said, her eyes smiling and teasing him. There was something about him; as dangerous as she knew him to be, she couldn't help being drawn to him, teasing him. Hopefully, he had no idea how deep her feelings for him were; hopefully, he thought she was only flirting, too.

Neville dropped her hand and executed an elegant bow. "May I have the privilege of standing up with you for this next dance?" he intoned for anyone to hear before adding softly, "My dear Lady Fairfax."

Annabelle's heart seemed suddenly to be beating in time with the opening chords of the music. Unable to speak, she swept him a curtsey and surrendered with a nod.

Neville's control was tested as he took Annabelle in his arms. His desire to clasp her tightly to his chest was almost overwhelming; her hand stole around his neck, and with the hand that rested on her waist, his thumb stroked her back gently.

"If I stopped here and kissed you, could you find it in your heart to forgive me?" he said, his eyes smiling down at her.

"I thought my heart was skipping beats," whispered Annabelle, trying for a light teasing tone. Undoubtedly, she was unsuccessful as she added breathlessly, "but now I think it has completely stopped."

With a laugh of sheer joy, Neville swept her into a dizzying turn. Giving up any pretense of flirtation, Annabelle leaned back in his arms, her laughter rippling through the notes of the music.

With an exuberance borne of love, they floated through the movements of the waltz. Words were unnecessary as their gazes locked, the warmth written plainly in their eyes.

Phoebe missed her steps more than once as her first sanctioned waltz proceeded. Twisting her head and trying to aim their steps toward her mother, she came down squarely on Lord West's instep, causing him to yelp in protest.

"Here now, I thought you said you could perform the waltz, Phoebe."

"What?" she said, dragging her attention back to her partner. "Well, of course I can! Don't be absurd!"

"Then what is the matter?"

"What indeed?" she said, frowning at her mother in Sir Neville's arms.

Annabelle and Neville, oblivious to the stares and comments their unbridled waltz was causing, were surprised and disappointed when the music ended. Reluctantly, Neville dropped his hands to his side.

Leaning close to her ear, he whispered, "The Robertsons have a lovely garden, I am told."

"Give me fifteen minutes." She didn't care if it was only a flirtation on his part; she would enjoy this evening without regret. For tonight, she would play the coquette for him, she decided as she delivered a deep curtsey along with a wicked smile and wink.

Annabelle drifted away, willing her high color to recede as she greeted other guests with a nonchalance she didn't feel.

I am mad, she told herself as she progressed to the ladies withdrawing room to bathe her face. This is not the reason I have come to London. He's only engaging in a light flirtation. This means nothing to him; he does this all the time. I should remember this is only a

diversion for him until Lady Rand-Smythe or some other
sophisticate appears.

"May I be of assistance, my lady?"

Annabelle glanced in the mirror to see the reflection
of a young abigail behind her. Realizing she had been
sitting for five minutes or more without so much as
patting her hair, Annabelle shook her head and rose.

"No, I have everything I need." Taking a coin out of
her reticule and handing it to the maid, Annabelle
added softly, "Absolutely everything."

Chapter Eight

Neville left the dance floor and immediately made his way to the balcony. It was narrow, only the width of the town house, but it led into a dark garden dotted by paper lanterns swaying in the gentle breeze.

He took out his watch, snapped it closed, and tapped his foot impatiently.

"What, exactly, was that all about?" demanded Phoebe, tugging at his sleeve.

"Not now, Phoebe," he said, turning to face her.

"You make a spectacle of my mother, and you refuse to discuss it? I think an explanation is in order."

Her indignation would have been amusing if he weren't expecting her mother to appear at any moment. So Neville reviewed his options. With Phoebe, there was the choice of an all-out row, fabrication of a lie, or complete capitulation in which he divulged his love for her mother. The last was hardly a choice since he had not yet told her mother of his desires. The first wasn't possible. They were much too close to the house. So, a lie it must be. He wondered if falsehoods came more easily with practice.

"If you must know, I was trying to better understand your mother so that I might help you choose the best possible husband for her. I had to discover what sort of things make her laugh, what makes her . . . herself!"

"Oh, I suppose that makes sense."

"Of course it does. You said yourself I should be able to come up with some candidates since I know everyone in London."

"Yes, that's true."

"But that's only half the story. I have to know the sort of man your mother might like. And for that, I must become better acquainted with her."

"Oh, I'm sorry; I suppose I misjudged you."

"No apology necessary. You are concerned for her well-being, and that is understandable after the near-miss with Duncan."

Phoebe shuddered, and Neville added, "You must go back inside; you'll catch a chill and then where will we be?"

Phoebe pressed his hand, grinning up at him in a conspiratorial manner before following his suggestion and returning to the house.

Annabelle stepped out from the shadows and walked slowly toward him.

"You came," he said, smiling at her.

Another couple strolled onto the balcony, and Neville led Annabelle down the steps. When he would have gone farther, she balked.

"What is it?"

"What were you talking to my daughter about?"

"Your daughter?"

"Yes, you and she seemed quite intimate a few moments ago."

"Intimate?" he echoed, playing for time. "Not at all. She had come out for a breath of fresh air, and I merely advised her that she shouldn't leave the ballroom unaccompanied." When Annabelle didn't respond, he laughed and added, "She, of course, felt compelled to tell me to mind my own business."

"That's not how it looked when she took your hand."

"She . . . ? No, I took her hand to lead her back inside, but she said she could manage by herself. She's quite independent, isn't she?"

Annabelle smiled. "That is an understatement of the grossest magnitude."

"But I didn't ask you here to . . ."

The other couple started down the steps, and Neville guided Annabelle farther into the garden.

When they were quite secluded, he took her hands and turned her to face him.

"You look beautiful tonight," he whispered.

Annabelle gave him a half-smile, and Neville added hastily, "You always look beautiful, but tonight, especially so."

"You needn't pay me empty compliments, Sir Neville."

"Empty? I don't know if you are being dishonest with yourself or begging for more, my dear."

Yes, this is a flirtation, thought Annabelle. In London, this was the sort of exchange that passed for conversation when one engaged in a flirtation. She tried to think of some witty rejoinder, but a cloud had covered her heart, and she remained silent.

"Have I said something to upset you? You look unhappy all of a sudden," said Neville, his long fingers tilting her face up to meet his. Annabelle didn't resist, and his lips touched hers. His arms slipped around her, gently pulling her petite frame against him.

This, thought Annabelle, is not a dream; it is nothing like, and she responded in a manner long since forgotten. Her arms circled his neck, and she pressed her body along the entire length of his. His mouth moved to her neck and along the swell of her breast before returning to capture her lips again.

Annabelle's fingers twisted in his dark hair, and she moaned into his mouth, her tongue meeting his. Neville felt the blood surging, his control slipping, and would have taken her then and there. But with no sofa, no bed, not so much as a stone bench, the futility of their situation managed to reach through his passion to his common sense.

"Annabelle," he breathed, clinging to her, his lips resting against her hair as rational thought slowly returned.

Releasing her enough to look down, he lifted her chin again. Her eyes were closed tightly, and he saw a thin trickle of tears escaping, descending slowly down her cheeks.

"What is it, dearest?" he asked, smiling to find her overcome by their lovemaking.

Annabelle shook her head, her fist coming to her mouth to stifle a sob. The expression of pain in her eyes was evident even in the darkened garden, and Neville stepped back in surprise. Annabelle fled.

His shock evaporated, and he started after her, but he was too late. When he reached the balcony, she was gone. He strode inside, glaring at the guests in the ballroom, but she was nowhere in sight.

Neville's fierce scowl cleared a passageway through the crowded room as he made his way to the front door and outside, into the darkness. With a curse, he went back inside and climbed the steps two at a time to the chamber set aside for the ladies. His entrance was greeted with shrill exclamations, but Annabelle was not within. He left the room, stopping outside the door, his mien dejected; she had vanished.

On the terrace, Annabelle stepped away from the shadows. Standing close to the doors, she hailed a passing footman.

"Is there another way into the house?" she asked, her tear-stained face requiring no further explanation.

Once inside, she sent for the carriage, leaving a note for Margaret, telling her she had been overcome by the heat and had gone home early.

The carriage ride was accomplished in grim-faced oblivion. Annabelle waited until she had gained the privacy of her room, waited until her maid had dressed her for bed and blown out the candles, before the floodgate of tears opened.

Idiotish, feminine fool! she whispered between sobs. How could I have been so stupid? Why did I ever consent to dance with him?

When she had recovered enough to be rational, she told herself firmly, only a schoolgirl would allow herself to fall in love with a worthless tulip of the Ton, a here and therein, a . . . If only he weren't so handsome . . . If only he didn't possess such a dear smile . . . If only his dark eyes didn't set free a flurry of butterflies in her stomach every time she beheld him!

But they do. He does, she reminded herself. And you have had the misfortune to fall head over heels in love with Sir Neville Colston. And because of that, you must avoid him; you must deny his very existence! It will be difficult, but not beyond your capabilities.

Oh, if only I could go home, whispered the thready voice of despair.

* * *

"I will run away to a convent!" wailed Charlotte, throwing herself, face down, on the bed.

The morning sun shone brightly through the window, but the occupants of the bedchamber were in varying degrees of distress. Mr. Sinclair's call on Lord Sweet had not gone well; he had been sent about his business, and only Charlotte's mother was pleased with the outcome.

Phoebe, who had never felt the pangs of love, was having difficulty empathizing with her friend. Sensibly, she responded, "You would have to go to France to join a convent, Charlotte, and you don't even speak French!"

"Phoebe!" exclaimed her mother, patting Charlotte on the back as the girl got her second wind. "Please, my dear, don't take on so. It may seem unbearable at the moment, Charlotte, but you will come about—in time."

"I don't want to 'come about'! I want to marry Sinbad!"

"I don't see why you cannot. I thought your Papa liked him," said Phoebe.

"He . . . he does! But Mama does not!" cried Charlotte, falling back onto the counterpane and sobbing loudly.

"And why not, pray tell," said Phoebe. "I mean, your dowry could easily support the two of you. It's not as if you would starve. If he really cares about you, he'll carry you off to Gretna Green or something," she added, warming to this adventurous idea.

Annabelle turned and glared at her daughter. "You are not helping matters, Phoebe. Charlotte may not understand her parents' objections, but she must honor them. I think you should run along."

"But this is my room!" complained Phoebe. Her mother raised her left brow, and Phoebe shook her head and flounced out of the room, leaving the comforting of Charlotte to her mother.

Charlotte continued to cry for some time. Annabelle handed her fresh handkerchiefs when the one in Charlotte's clenched fingers became limp and damp. She patted Charlotte's back and murmured platitudes which had no effect whatsoever on the distraught girl.

All the while, Annabelle was wondering what her old friend was about to make her daughter suffer so. Surely Mr. Sinclair was not so objectionable. He had a comfortable income and an estate, albeit a tiny one. Had Phoebe's heart led her to one such as Mr. Sinclair, she would have been content. As for Margaret's objection that Mr. Sinclair was a member of the Corinthian set and a gambler, she had seen no evidence of it since he had met Charlotte. And he was so considerate; what other man would accompany three ladies shopping without a single complaint? If that did not prove his devotion, then nothing could.

Annabelle kept such thoughts to herself, of course. But as she cradled Charlotte in her arms, she was thankful her own daughter was not suffering from the trauma of unfulfilled love.

"It's her mother, you know. I tell you, Neville, if she were a man, I would challenge her to a duel!" declared Sinbad, his usual genial personality overshadowed by his morning visit with Lord Sweet.

"A duel with your future mother-in-law?" said Neville, accepting the fresh cup of coffee a footman presented to him. Buttering another piece of toast, he said, "Come here and share a cup of coffee with me."

Sinbad ignored this invitation and jumped to his feet, almost knocking over his chair. Banging his fist on the mahogany table, he proclaimed, "I would at least plant her a facer."

"Why don't you challenge your older brother instead; were you the viscount with a large property, her ladyship couldn't object," said Neville, the absurdity of this suggestion lost on his tormented friend.

"Perhaps that would have worked three nephews ago, Nev, but I draw the line at infanticide," said Sinbad, his usual ready smile weak and drawn. Righting his chair, he sank into it and buried his face in his hands for several moments. When he spoke, his voice was forlorn. "I tell you, Nev, I feel I'll go mad if—"

"Let me speak to Lady Fairfax. She has a great deal of influence on her old friend. Perhaps she will intervene on your behalf. You said she seemed to be promoting your suit."

"I thought so, but I have begun to doubt my judgment," said the younger man with a desolate laugh.

"Chin up, Sinbad. You know the saying: Unlucky at cards, lucky in love. I would say you're a sure thing at this love business."

Sir Neville left his friend sitting disconsolate in his dining room and ordered his curricle brought round. Aside from his promise to Sinbad, he wanted very badly to seek an explanation from Annabelle about her distress the night before. He had kissed many females in his life, but he had yet to make one cry with a simple kiss. And the pain in her eyes . . . It was a mystery he couldn't fathom.

It was the wrong time of the day to call, of course, being the hour when the rest of the Ton rose and paid duty calls to each other. He only hoped he would be able to see Annabelle alone.

Neville's luck was quite out; there were a half-dozen guests before him. His attempts to entice her away from the crowd were thwarted by a particularly annoying Mr. Duncan, who refused to leave Annabelle's side.

He found an ally in Phoebe, who tried to distract Duncan, while giving Neville a significant look and rolling her eyes, indicating she required his assistance in getting rid of the scoundrel. Neville, however, couldn't devise a plan; his anger at witnessing Duncan's attentions to Annabelle and her appearance of pleasure from this were making rational thought impossible. Frustrated, Neville soon departed, sympathizing heartily with Sinbad's desire to call someone out.

All in all, the day had been a complete disaster. Seeing Annabelle, a tiny crease in her brow and her conversation distracted, had awakened in him a desire to protect her, to comfort her. He found, however, that one niggling doubt remained to haunt him, and the possibility that she did not hold him in very high regard was almost intolerable. He understood perfectly Sinbad's threat to run away to Gretna Green and be married over the anvil. He would do the same, if only he could be certain Annabelle would have him.

That had been the unanswerable question since the previous night in the garden. Having to deal with the mundane tasks of living—dressing, eating, sleeping—filled him with an almost uncontrollable desire to act, even if his actions proved disastrous. So he held a tight rein on his inclinations and tried to lose himself in his painting. For the first time in Neville's well-ordered life, this proved impossible.

* * *

To no avail had Annabelle pled Mr. Sinclair's case to her friend. All Margaret would say was that Charlotte could do much better. Though Annabelle's persuasive powers were great, her friend was adamant.

In the days that followed, however, it became obvious to everyone that Charlotte was not doing better at all. Her tears were dry, but her gaze was hollow, and even a planned picnic in the country with Mr. Good and Lord West in attendance did not bring the bloom back to her cheeks.

When they returned after this outing, Lady Margaret said, "I am very much afraid I shall have to send Charlotte to her Great Aunt Hildegard."

"And that is supposed to cheer her?" asked Annabelle.

"I daresay nothing could cheer her, but she needn't cast the entire household into the doldrums. And you, dear Annabelle, you must think of Phoebe; she is still very much in demand. We mustn't allow Charlotte's histrionics to spoil Phoebe's chances."

Annabelle, who had begun to think Phoebe would be going home at the end of the Season heart-whole and happy about it, said reasonably, "You cannot expect Phoebe to allow Charlotte to go alone. Perhaps another week or two will see Charlotte's spirits on the mend."

Margaret was noncommittal, her silence allowing Annabelle the time to consider her own affairs. These reflections did little to cheer her.

When Sir Neville had called, she had been engaged in conversation with Mr. Duncan. She still couldn't decide if this had been for the best or not. She felt altogether undisciplined where Sir Neville was concerned. Indeed, when he had called, she had wanted only to go to him, to kiss him, to reveal her passion for him. And had she succumbed to this desire? Sir Neville would have been appalled, she felt sure. His anger that afternoon had been palpable, and since then he had been conspicuously absent from the Sweets' town house.

As for Mr. Duncan, that gentleman had positively haunted the drawing room for the past week. He had, in short, worn out his welcome with Annabelle. He was kind enough, but she had discovered that kindness became dull after daily contact. Not that she wanted him to, but he had not so much as attempted to hold her hand. Unlike Neville, he was too much of a gentleman.

Since they had put about the story that Charlotte was ill, they had not attended many social functions, only an intimate card party and a musicale given by one of the other political hostesses. But Charlotte was now officially "well" since she had attended the picnic.

And now, Annabelle knew she could no longer avoid contact with Sir Neville. She both dreaded and longed for the opportunity to see him again. Would he speak to her? He certainly hadn't sought her out; evidently he had no trouble being parted from her, another piece of evidence that his kiss had only been a part of his flirtation. The kiss had meant nothing to him. To Annabelle, it had meant the world.

Chapter Nine

The evening brought a chilly rain, quite in keeping with the somber gatherings in the dining rooms at the town houses of Sir Neville and Lord Sweet. Sinbad had spent the day moping about the library, his sighs irritating Neville, who didn't have the heart to send him about his business. At Lord Sweet's table, one chair was empty, Charlotte having finally been sent to bed with a dose of laudanum.

Lord Sweet had agreed to accompany the other ladies to the theater. Annabelle was not in the mood, but the play was Shakespeare's tragedy of love, *Romeo and Juliet*, so she thought she could tolerate it. Phoebe, too, was subdued without Charlotte's presence.

Sir Neville had also persuaded his sullen friend to go to the theater and was putting the finishing touches on his cravat. Sinbad sat on the edge of a chair by the door, his chin resting on his walking stick. His coat was wrinkled and his hair untidy.

Neville searched for a subject that might produce

some sort of reaction. Finally, he stepped back from the mirror and said,"I don't think I quite have the hang of this mathematical. You do it much better than I."

"Humph," grumbled Sinclair.

"You know, if only you would go to Almack's, you might find someone else to court, now that you have the hang of it."

His expression incredulous, Sinbad shot back, "You really have no idea what it is to be in love, do you, Neville? I care only for Charlotte; no one else will do."

Neville's patience snapped. "You know, Sinbad, you are not the only one to suffer from unrequited love," he said, close to revealing his own unsettled predicament. Instead, he continued in generalities. "There are thousands of other people in this world suffering at this very moment, but they are not so blasted annoying about it."

Sinclair looked up, his eyes as mournful as a hound dog, and he said softly, "Sorry, Neville. Maybe I should just go back home."

Neville grimaced, feeling like someone who had just kicked a whimpering dog, but he said firmly, "Not on your life! Get on your feet. You're going to the play! And if Miss Sweet happens to be in attendance, you will *not* fall prostrate at her feet."

Lord Sweet's party had not been seated five minutes when Mr. Duncan made an appearance at the door to their box. Lady Margaret welcomed him warmly, turning to Annabelle and Phoebe to second her comments.

"Good evening, sir," said Phoebe.

"Good evening. What a pleasant surprise," said Annabelle, throwing a suspicious glance at her old friend. Margaret winked and moved over one chair to allow

Mr. Duncan to occupy the seat beside her old friend. Annabelle wanted to scream with frustration. She would have words with Margaret later!

For a quarter of an hour, Annabelle responded with an occasional grunt to Mr. Duncan's running dialogue on the history of the playhouse. She reflected sourly that he now felt quite comfortable in her company; no shyness remained to make him careful of his conversation. He felt free to bore her to death.

Annabelle diverted her thoughts by raising her opera glasses and studying the audience as they waited for the curtains to go up. The bottom floor was like a restless sea undulating with movement and conversation. Lifting her glasses, she surveyed the boxes lining the opposite side of the theater.

There he was, sitting beside a forlorn-looking Mr. Sinclair. Annabelle felt her heart swell with emotion. It was as if she had only been marking time over the last week, waiting for him to reappear, to complete her, to bring her back to life.

He nodded, smiling across the wide expanse of the crowded theater. Without thinking, Annabelle lifted her small, gloved hand and waved.

She watched as he said something to the glum Sinclair and then rose. He made a little circular motion with his hand and left the box.

Annabelle, who had never practiced the art of deception, said weakly, "Oh, I do believe I'm going to be ill. That leg of lamb, Margaret, I thought it tasted strange."

"We should go," said Lord Sweet, starting to rise before Annabelle waved him back down.

"No, I shall be fine. I must get out of this box. There is simply no air up here. If I get a breath of air, I'll feel fine, I'm sure."

"Allow me to accompany you," said Duncan.

"No!" said Phoebe and Annabelle simultaneously.

"That is, Phoebe may accompany me. I feel the need of feminine support. I know you understand." Annabelle rose, giving Duncan no chance to dispute his understanding. Phoebe followed, her hand on her mother's elbow.

When they had moved away from the box, Annabelle whispered, "Really, Phoebe, you may return to the box. I will be fine."

"Then you're not ill?" asked Phoebe. She grinned when her mother shook her head. "Couldn't take any more of Mr. Duncan's lecture?"

"I know it is unkind; I know he is a worthy man, but I cannot like him."

"He is not so worthy," muttered Phoebe.

"What was that?" asked Annabelle.

"Nothing, nothing. I suppose we should be returning," said Phoebe morosely.

"Yes, you should, but I need to . . . I'll be back in a few moments. Tell them I am fine," said Annabelle, her eyes widening slightly when she saw Neville striding down the passageway. Spying Phoebe suddenly, he ducked into an alcove.

When Phoebe had disappeared, Annabelle hurried down the hall to meet him. Neville took her hands in his, pulling her close so he could study her expression, her beauty.

"I have missed you," she said, wishing he would return the compliment.

Instead, Neville opened a door and ushered her into a dark room, a storage closet, judging from the crates and brooms. A single window high on the far wall provided a hint of light.

Without a word, Neville took her into his arms and kissed her thoroughly. When Annabelle would have spoken, he placed a long finger on her lips, shaking his head and bending his head to kiss her again.

His lips blazed a trail of fire as they descended to her neck. His hand cupped one breast, his lips teasing it free of its restraints. Annabelle gasped, holding his head to guide him, and thrust her hips against him. He answered in kind, his movements awakening in them both powerful, unconstrained lust.

"We must go somewhere . . ." he breathed raggedly, his lips leaving her exposed flesh.

Annabelle, incapable of speech, whimpered into his tangled hair and pressed closer.

A small laugh escaped his lips, and Neville raised his mouth to hers, soothing her with a long, deep kiss.

Lifting his head finally, he teased, "Can't stand to do without me long enough to find a bed?"

Annabelle frowned, her hazy thoughts slowly processing his words. Somehow, they didn't sound like words of love—passion, perhaps, but not love. Neville's tongue erased all thought as he kissed her again.

At length, he lifted his head, his hands gently pulling her bodice back in place, smoothing the fabric covering her breasts with his thumbs, torturing her nipples with a last caress.

"When can you come to me?" he whispered, kissing the tip of her nose.

His question caused alarms to sound in Annabelle's head as her unbridled ardor receded. "I don't know what you mean," she whispered miserably, wishing she truly did not know the meaning of his words.

"Annabelle, I want you," said Neville, his arms pulling her roughly against him again. "And I think you want me."

The door was pushed open, and Neville was dragged into the glaring light.

"What the blazes . . . ?" exclaimed Neville.

Annabelle listened in horror as a long catalog of invectives issued from the mouth of the saintly Mr. Duncan, ending with a fist crashing into Neville's jaw.

Jumping up and down, Phoebe grabbed Duncan's arm at the same time as Neville retaliated with a punishing right which glanced off Duncan's ear and clipped Phoebe's temple, sending her sprawling.

"Phoebe, good God!" exclaimed Neville, pushing Duncan away with one arm and dropping to the ground, lifting the stunned Phoebe in his arms.

Several spectators appeared at the doorways of their boxes, and Duncan had the presence of mind to say loudly, "It must have been the heat. Don't worry, my lady, we will see you and your daughter home safely."

"Thank you," said Annabelle, pushing the closet door closed with her foot as she automatically followed his lead. "If you don't mind, Sir Neville, would you tell Lord Sweet about Phoebe and explain that we have gone home early?" she said, having the presence of mind to leave Neville to tell the story instead of the outraged Mr. Duncan. He might tell Margaret much more than she wished for her friend to hear.

"Annabelle," Neville protested, frowning sternly.

"Please," she breathed, looking at him with love and sorrow.

"Of course. Tell Phoebe . . . I'm sorry," he added, placing Phoebe carefully in Duncan's waiting arms.

"Thank you, Sir Neville," said Annabelle, resisting the desire to kiss him goodbye.

Annabelle settled back in the carriage, Phoebe's head resting in her lap. Duncan, his jaw still set in anger, studied them in silence.

Coming out of her swoon, Phoebe whispered, "Sir Neville?"

"*Shh*, my love. We will be home soon. Mr. Duncan has been so kind as to see us home in his carriage." Annabelle smiled at him, but his expression remained stern.

"Duncan?" said Phoebe, struggling to sit up. "No! Not him, Mother!"

"*Shh*, Phoebe! You mustn't speak of Mr. Duncan like that, said Annabelle, giving the gentleman a rueful smile. "She's out of her head."

"She is not alone, I think," he said coldly.

"What is that supposed to mean?" asked Annabelle, wishing immediately she had not given him an opening to censure her actions.

"If you must know, my lady, I find your behavior demonstrates that you are lacking in the qualities that I consider requisite for a lady—any lady, much less my wife."

"I don't recall applying for the position of your wife, sir," declared Annabelle. "Furthermore, I didn't ask for your endorsement of my behavior. You may be a gentleman, but—"

"Gentleman? Ha!" said Phoebe, struggling to sit up straight before falling back weakly into her mother's arms.

"What's that supposed to mean?" asked her audience.

"A rake and a rogue," she mumbled, closing her eyes and leaving them to glare at each other in the dim light of the carriage.

"We're here," said Duncan.

"So we are," responded Annabelle haughtily.

"I shall see you safely inside," he added.

Annabelle looked up to see the butler sending two

footmen down the steps. "Thank you, sir, but there is no need. Help me with Miss Phoebe, Robert; she fainted and fell."

"Very good, my lady," said the young man, shouldering past Duncan.

"Goodbye, Mr. Duncan," said Annabelle with a note of finality in her voice.

By the time Annabelle had seen Phoebe settled in her bed and had hurriedly changed into her own wrapper, the bump beside Phoebe's eye had grown considerably and had turned a deep purple.

Mary, who had been on their estate, clucked around the room nervously, building up the fire, offering her mistress a glass of sherry, straightening the covers. Finally, Annabelle sent her away, preferring solitude to watch Phoebe sleep.

Charlotte, her own eyes swollen with a recent bout of tears, heard of the mishap and rushed to Phoebe's side. Between her tears and self-tortured "If only I had been there" 's, she soon had Annabelle urging her to go back to her room in order to save her strength for later visits, when Phoebe might need entertaining.

"Might need? Do you mean she might not . . . Is she going to die?" wailed Charlotte.

"Good heavens, no! That is not at all what I meant!" Annabelle ushered Charlotte to the door, saying gently, "I only meant tomorrow when she is better, she will need you much more than she needs me. Now go to bed, Charlotte. Phoebe will be right as rain on the morrow." She kissed Charlotte's cheek and closed the door firmly behind her.

Annabelle sighed in frustration when the door opened only moments later, but it was Margaret, coming

in to exclaim in surprise and concern over both Annabelle and Phoebe.

"For you must know, Annabelle, when I sent Mr.
Duncan out to discover what had happened to you, I
had no intention of letting Phoebe out of my sight. But
she insisted. And now this. Imagine my surprise when
Sir Neville Colston came in and told us what had happened!"

"I suppose," said Annabelle, crossing her fingers in
the folds of her wrapper, "Phoebe was feeling poorly
to begin with and hoped some fresh air might revive
her."

"I suppose," said Margaret doubtfully. "Sir Neville
tried to explain how she had hit her head when she
fainted, but he made very little sense."

"How was the play?" asked Annabelle quickly. "Did
you enjoy it?"

"It was all very well," she replied. "Though you know
I enjoy the farce above all, but we thought it best to
return home to check on you both. Wherever did you
get to, Annabelle?"

"Me? Oh, I was talking to an acquaintance, and I
forgot about the time."

Margaret leaned over and placed a hand on Phoebe's
brow. "Has she opened her eyes at all?"

"Yes, twice, but it seems to tire her, and then she
goes back to sleep. I shall probably send for the surgeon
tomorrow."

"I think we should. She would probably benefit from
a letting."

"Not that," said Annabelle decisively. "But I would
feel better if the physician examined this bruise. You
should go on to bed, Margaret. I'm going to sit up with
her."

"I would tell you to let the maid do that," said Marga-

ret, "but I know how it is when one's child is unwell."
Kissing her fingertips to Annabelle, she gathered steam
and sailed away.

Annabelle blew out all the candles except one and
sat back in the chair by the bed, pulling a lap rug over
her knees.

Phoebe slept quietly for several hours. Annabelle, lay-
ing her head on her folded arms on the side of the
bed, slept fitfully. She was too tired to think about anything, even Neville.

The dawn's light was filtering through the curtains
when Annabelle awoke, the touch of someone's hand
on her shoulder rousing her. She lifted her head and
smiled.

"You're awake. How do you feel?"

Phoebe didn't try to sit up, but she smiled weakly and
whispered, "I'll live."

Sitting up straight and stretching, Annabelle asked
briskly, "Now, what can I do for you? Would you like
something to drink?"

"First things first," said Phoebe, struggling up on her
elbows. With a grimace, she fell back against the pillows.

"Try not to move too fast, my love. You may be dizzy
for several days."

Annabelle began to move about the room nervously.
Memories of her passionate encounter, of what Phoebe
must have seen, flooded her thoughts, and her face
grew hot and flushed.

"Charlotte came by last night; she'll be delighted you
are still among the living," said Annabelle with a forced
laugh. "Lady Margaret also checked on you. Ah, here
is Mary with some hot chocolate. I'll just go to my room
to change now."

"Mother," said Phoebe, her voice already stronger than before.

"We'll talk when I return. Drink your chocolate."

Annabelle hurried away, arriving at her own room, where she closed and locked the door.

"That will help," she said, her voice heavy with self-mockery, and she retraced her steps and unlocked the door before she went to the dressing table and sank down on the narrow bench.

What must Phoebe think of me? What can I say to excuse myself? Annabelle demanded of the weary face staring back at her. She discovers her mother in a torrid embrace, practically . . . No, I had my clothes on; Neville had already pulled my dress back up. But what about him? I do hope Phoebe didn't notice or understand the state he was in; Duncan certainly had, but as a gentleman, he should keep his mouth closed. Neville, of course, wouldn't say anything—not about the woman he . . .

Annabelle sat taller and frowned. Loved? she wondered. He had never said he loved her; he hadn't even said he missed her. She searched her memory for his exact words. "I want you." Her face flamed anew when she recalled the way he had laughed when she had as good as begged him not to stop. What had he said? Something about her not being able to wait until they could get in bed.

"My God," she whispered.

"Mother."

"Phoebe! You shouldn't be out of bed! Come here and sit down." Annabelle led Phoebe to a comfortable chair and returned to the bench, watching her daughter in the mirror.

"I have a confession to make, Mother."

"You?"

"Yes, and if I could take it all back, I would. It is all my fault!" she said, bursting into noisy sobs.

Annabelle flew to her daughter's side and, kneeling beside the chair, put her arms around her.

"There now, don't distress yourself so! Nothing you could have done is as bad as all that! Whatever it is, we'll make it right."

Annabelle produced a serviceable handkerchief and put it up to Phoebe's nose. "Here now, blow your nose."

Phoebe obeyed, and bowed her head, still sniffling, her bottom lip trembling.

"You may not say that after you hear, Mother. It is Sir Neville. Well, partly it is about him, but I started it."

An uneasiness gripped Annabelle, but she urged Phoebe to continue.

"When we first arrived in London, I felt so hemmed in by all the rules. I know you warned me, but it was so difficult. And then, all the ladies would tease me about finding a husband. I mean, I know that's what the Season is all about, but I didn't want to think about that. I wasn't interested in marriage yet. Even you kept going on about my finding a husband." She took a deep breath.

"All Charlotte and I really wanted was adventure— the type of adventure young ladies weren't supposed to have."

"I do seem to recall a few incidents," said Annabelle dryly.

"Yes, well, perhaps we shouldn't delve too deeply into that subject," said Phoebe with a weak smile. "Actually, you know most of it. Charlotte and I are either very bad at deception, or you are very, very observant."

"A little of both, I should think."

"Yes, but we decided . . . that is, we devised a plan to occupy your time so we could enjoy ourselves."

"A plan," echoed Annabelle warily.

"Yes, it seemed such a good idea at the time."

Her daughter fell silent, and Annabelle prompted her.

"What? Oh yes, well, we decided we would find *you* a husband."

"You what!" exclaimed Annabelle, jumping up and striding away before turning back and staring incredulously.

"Don't worry, Mother," said Phoebe, "It wasn't like I placed an advertisement in the *Morning Post!*" Phoebe laughed at her own wit and continued with more enthusiasm. "I had to do it alone, as it turned out, since Charlotte was so wrapped up with Mr. Sinclair. But I danced with all the candidates to determine if they were, well, good enough for you. That wasn't enough, however. I mean, I thought Mr. Duncan was an excellent prospect until I found out he . . . Well, I'm not sure what he does, but it is something that would be unsuitable for me to hear about! So what was I to do? As your daughter, I couldn't very well demand to know their financial and family circumstances."

"Of course not," said Annabelle weakly, walking back and collapsing onto the ottoman at Phoebe's feet. Like a child both enthralled and repelled by a ghost story, she returned for more.

"And then someone offered to take care of that for me, to determine if they were truly eligible."

Annabelle closed her eyes before asking, "And so you chose Sir Neville to be my husband."

"Sir Neville Colston? I should say not! Why, he is the last man I should want for a steppapa! I would never be able to get away with anything!"

Shaking her head in confusion, Annabelle said, "Then how does he enter into all of this?"

"It's simple. Sir Neville offered to find out each candidate's circumstances. It was he who volunteered to discover if the men I chose were suitable or not."

Horrified, Annabelle covered her face.

"It didn't really work out as he said, however. He was always dancing with you, and when I demanded to know why, he told me it was so he could get to know you better in order to be able to help me decide on who, in the Ton, might be the best match for you."

"Phoebe, you didn't!"

"When he said it, it seemed like a good idea," she whined, raising her hands in supplication.

But Annabelle was looking inward and didn't notice. "What must he think of us?" she cried.

Phoebe drew herself up indignantly and declared, "The better question is what do we think of him? How dare he kiss you! And in a broom closet! There was no need for him to get to know you that well!"

Annabelle cut her off, saying sternly, "Go to your room now. I don't want to hear another word about any of this. And don't you dare breathe a word of it to anyone, not even Charlotte."

Phoebe's eyes grew round. "Yes, Mother," she said quietly. At the door, she paused and added, "I'm sorry if I spoiled your ... friendship with Sir Neville. But really, Mother, he was only using both of us. He is not worthy of you."

Annabelle felt her world crashing down around her. Not only was Sir Neville not in love with her, he had made her a figure of fun. And how many others had he told? Was her name and her daughter's being bandied about in the clubs, their names written in the wager books?

How he must have laughed when I surrendered to him!

"Oh, Lord," she whispered, almost swooning with embarrassment, "he did laugh!"

Tears were not normally a refuge for Lady Annabelle Fairfax. She rarely indulged her feelings with hysteria. But this fiasco was so unexpected, so devastating, that she allowed the tears to escape, falling unheeded down her cheeks.

When she had finished, she bathed her face and rang for hot water. Scrubbing her body vigorously, she tried to wash away her embarrassment, her anger, and her regret.

"Mary," she said when she was dressed in a cheerful yellow morning gown. "I am going home for a few days."

"When will you leave, my lady?"

"Early tomorrow morning. Until then, I have the headache and don't wish to be disturbed."

"Certainly, my lady," said the maid, clearing away the soap and towels.

"Oh, and Mary, you need only pack for two or three days; I have clothes at home to wear."

"Did you want me to accompany you, my lady?"

Annabelle patted the maid's hand and shook her head. "I know it is a great deal to ask, but would you please stay and keep an eye on Miss Phoebe?"

"Anything you wish, my lady."

"If only everything were as easy as that," murmured Annabelle.

Chapter Ten

For Sir Neville Colston, female conquests had never presented much of a challenge. Even as a youth, they had flocked to him. As a soldier, wearing scarlet regimentals, he had continued to experience success. Therefore, when he called on Annabelle and was turned away with a cold "My lady is not receiving," he was puzzled. His query on the invalid met with much the same response: "Miss Fairfax is improving, but she is not receiving either."

When this occurred four days in a row, such rejection became increasingly intolerable. Even the highest stickler might forgive Sir Neville, perhaps, for thrusting his foot in the door, looking the startled butler in the eye, and saying haughtily, "I think, my good man, if you tell Lady Fairfax it is Sir Neville, she will see me."

On reflection, Neville decided it was the glint of amusement in the fellow's eye which made him grab the insolent butler by the collar and shake him. Still, the man had insisted Lady Annabelle was not receiving.

Unwilling to admit defeat, Neville had gone around to the stables to ferret out any information there. His query about Phoebe's mare gave him the entrée into the groom's confidence, but the young man only shook his head and continued to polish a cumbersome traveling carriage.

"Don' know, guvner. Haven't seen any of th' ladies t'day. Someone took this carriage th' other day, but I couldn't say who. They always take it round t' the front door t' get in, you see."

"I see," said Neville, flicking a speck of dirt off the shiny black vehicle. "But someone went on a journey?" he asked with an inkling of suspicion raising its head.

"That's wot they tells me. Don' know who; they just said t' polish it up. That usually means someun is goin' somewhere. Then back it comes th' next day, an' they says to polish it up again."

"Thanks," said Neville, flipping a coin into the groom's hand, before he strode out of the stableyard.

"Damn her," he muttered, his anger growing as he stalked through the streets back to his house. Following him, keeping well behind so as to go unnoticed, was his tiger Antonio driving his grays.

When Neville entered his front door, the butler's surprise made him snap, "What are you gawking at? I do live here."

"Certainly, Sir Neville, but you usually drive up to the front step when you have left in your curricle. Ah, here it is now. I beg your pardon, sir."

Neville looked out the open door where Antonio grinned at him from the seat of his curricle.

"Blast!"

Neville pushed past the butler, who was still talking about something. The servant doggedly followed him into the library.

"What the devil do you want, Peters?" said Neville, stopping so short, the mortified butler stepped on his heel.

"He's just warning you that I'm in your library, drinking your port and eating your luncheon," said Sinbad Sinclair, looking over his shoulder from his seat on the leather sofa.

"Is that supposed to be news to me? Go away, Peters, and bring another bottle of port. This one isn't going to last very long," said Neville, shutting the door on the servant before dropping into a chair and stretching his long legs out before him.

"The female of our species is without a doubt the most vexing of God's creatures, Sinbad."

"I wouldn't say that," protested the younger man.

"Ah, but that, my friend, is because you are blinded by that equally vexing concept—love. And since her parents have forbidden your union, you have formed this high ideal of your lady love. You have placed her on a pedestal. You neither know nor care what she is truly like."

Sinbad handed him a full glass of port and shook his head.

"Ah, you scoff, but it is true," said Neville.

The door opened and the butler brought in a full bottle of port to replenish the decanter on the table beside the sofa.

"We'll just ask Peters. Tell me, Peters, do you not find the female of our species the most unpredictable, irritating creature on this earth?"

"I wouldn't know, sir."

"Why not? You have to work with the things," said Neville, emptying his glass and handing it to the butler for a refill.

"As you say, sir, but being in my position, I find it

much easier to leave the overseeing of the female staff to Mrs. Cook."

"Clever man!" said Neville, downing the second glass, letting its warmth sink in before once again handing the empty vessel to his butler for more. "So, tell me, how do you deal with Mrs. Cook? She's one of them, too, you know."

"I am aware of that, sir, but I believe she is a sensible female. That is, most of the time, she is sensible," added the butler.

"Aha! You see, Sinbad, even the most sensible one in the world will suffer occasional lapses!"

"But Neville, you, too, have occasional lapses!" laughed Sinbad. "Just look at you now."

The third glass was having its way with Neville, numbing his senses just as he had hoped. "Indeed," he said, his words slightly slurred, "just look at me now."

"Will that be all, Sir Neville?"

"What? Oh, of course. Thank you, Peters." As the butler closed the door, Neville added loudly, "And thank you for being a man!"

When Sinbad's laughter had subsided, he asked, "What has happened to set you off, old friend? I haven't seen you get this bosky, this fast, since the days after Waterloo."

"Ah, Waterloo. Now that was a time when a man could know what was expected of him. Kill the enemy. That's all you had to know."

"And stay alive," said Sinbad quietly, taking a large gulp from his glass.

"Yes, stay alive."

"Did you ever wonder what for, Nev?" asked Sinbad, straightening and leaning forward to tap his friend's foot to get his attention.

"What for?"

"Yes, why were we spared that day? Was it so we could come back here?"

"Hmm, I see what you mean. What for, indeed. Here we sit, blue-deviled and bewildered. There hardly seems to be any logic in that."

"Well, I'm not bewildered. I know I love Charlotte, and she loves me."

"Right," said Neville, sitting forward, frowning as he gathered his wits about him. "But to what end? Her parents won't have you. What are you going to do about it?"

"Do? What can a fellow do?" asked Sinbad, lying back on the sofa and gazing at the ceiling.

"There's always Gretna Green," said Neville, leaning back in his chair and closing his eyes.

In the comfortable elegance of the morning room at Fairbridge, her country home, Annabelle poured a second cup of tea for her visitors.

"I don't see how you could bear to leave town before the Season is over," said the squire's wife, taking yet another cherry tart.

"There's no mystery, Sally. I thought it best to come back now and check on the planting; it will do no harm if I miss a ball or two," said Annabelle, watching in amazement as Lady Shipton finished off the cherry tart and reached back for an apple tart.

"*Hmm,*" was all the response she could manage, but her married daughter took up the gauntlet and continued the interrogation.

"How would you say Society is this Season, Lady Fairfax? Is it a sad crush or rather thin this year?"

"I have no experience by which to judge, Madeline,

having never before journeyed to London," said Annabelle.

"Ah, I forgot. When I was there, the company was so gay; the ladies all dressed so beautifully, the men so elegant," said Madeline, essaying a haughty tone.

"Of course," murmured Annabelle. "But tell me how things are going here at home. I have missed everyone so much."

"Things are ever the same, my dear Annabelle," said the squire's lady. "We are working very hard to raise money for our school for the indigent. It has been a favorite project of yours, I know, and it seems to be slow-going since you left."

"Oh dear, what is the matter?" asked Annabelle, moving the empty plate away from her guest.

"It is the vicar," said the daughter. "The man is sitting on the money—if he has not absconded with it."

"Nonsense, Madeline. The vicar is an honorable man; he would never steal, especially from charity," said Annabelle.

Lady Shipton made an odd sucking noise with her teeth and pushed herself out of her chair. "I agree, Annabelle, but the man has not an original thought in his head. It is my belief he has been biding his time until your return so that you may tell him how best to spend the money."

"I?" said Annabelle, unwilling to acknowledge the truth of her ladyship's statement.

"Mark my words," said the squire's wife, giving Annabelle a peck on the cheek before saying to her daughter, "Come along, Madeline. We have two more calls to make."

Annabelle smiled, wondering how many more "light refreshments" her friend would make her way through before she finished her calls. It always amazed her how much food Sally Shipton downed and yet remained as thin as a reed. Her daughter Madeline was never seen eating so much as a grape, but she was twice her mother's size. Such an odd combination.

When her visitors had gone, Annabelle called for the pony trap to be brought around and put on her bonnet. She would need to get to the bottom of the school fund problem without delay. As much as she hated to admit it, she felt sure Sally had been in the right of it. Reginald Rutherford never made a move without checking with her. She was only thankful he didn't consult her on his sermons. He was really a powerful orator, very inspiring, but had he asked her, she would have informed him his sermons were about forty minutes too long.

She pulled the mare to a stop outside a large, white-washed cottage and climbed down. Giving the mare a carrot, she tied the ribbons to the gate post and walked up the carefully tended path to the front door.

It stood wide open, as usual, making Annabelle smile. She had asked Mr. Rutherford why he never closed his door, if he wasn't afraid of wild beasts or even a stray skunk, but he had told her heartily his door was always open to all of God's creatures. He was really a very kind man, despite the fact that Phoebe was correct in her assessment that he was a prosy bore.

He was also a handsome man, in a golden sort of way, thought Annabelle, as he greeted her heartily. Even as she was saying all the polite necessities, he fell short as she compared him to another figure—one much darker and dearer.

With a dazzling smile for the vicar, Annabelle dismissed Sir Neville from her mind and said, "Now that I am home, vicar, perhaps we can discuss the plans for our village school."

"Of course, dear lady, of course. We have enough

funds, I believe, to hire a teacher. I have debated on whether we should hire a man or a woman, since we hope some of our girls will also attend."

"That is a consideration," said Annabelle. "Do you also expect to help—with the classics, I mean. Several of our young men would benefit from some instruction in Greek and Latin."

He preened and agreed, saying pompously, "I don't want to put myself forward, my dear lady, but I excelled in both studies. However, do you believe farmers' lads have a need for such difficult subjects?"

"I think certain boys such as Farmer Johnson's son should certainly have the opportunity. He is very quick, and as he is the fourth son, I think he and his family would benefit from it. He could become a clerk at the very least, perhaps even a solicitor."

"Yes, yes, you are right, as usual, my lady. Very well, since I am quite capable of filling that need, then perhaps we should hire a female. She must be of the highest moral character," he said pompously.

"Yes, but not too old. A younger woman will have more patience with the little ones."

"Ah, now I might challenge you on that one, my dear Lady Fairfax. Only look at yourself. You were patience personified when you taught the little girls how to knit socks for charity."

"I bow to your opinion on that," said Annabelle, amused as always when he had made some gaff without even realizing it. She could not resist adding, "But not every older woman is as patient as I am."

"Older woman!" he exclaimed, turning pink. "Why, I never meant . . . You must believe, my lady, I had no intention of saying . . . That is, I didn't mean you were old!"

"Thank you, vicar, I was just having a bit of fun at your expense. Please forgive me," she said.

He shook his head mournfully and intoned in his sermonish best, "It is not becoming in one of your high social station to practice levity on those of us lower on the social register. Far be it from me to instruct you—"

"Of course," said Annabelle, rising hurriedly. "Now, I really must be going. You will start the search for a suitable teacher, won't you?"

"Well, I would prefer your assistance, my lady," said the vicar.

"I'm afraid I won't be around to help, Mr. Rutherford. I'm going back to London next week."

"That doesn't give us much time. I'll contact an agency immediately; perhaps we may have some applicants here before you leave. Or perhaps you may be able to interview them in London."

"Oh, I don't know about that," said Annabelle.

"I could journey there to help with the process," he said eagerly.

Annabelle shook her head. "No, you are needed here. If you will contact the agency, tell them they may send applicants to me in London. I will choose one, and she can then come here for your final approval."

"If you think that is best, my lady."

"It would be the most expedient way, I think. Now, I must be going. So good to see you again, Mr. Rutherford," said Annabelle, extending her hand.

Instead of the usual gentle shake, the vicar lifted her hand to his lips and kissed the back of her glove noisily. With a deep bow, he helped her into the dog cart, watching as she drove away.

* * *

Annabelle filled her mornings confering with her bailiff and inspecting the estate. In the afternoon she was either "at home" to receive calls or out making them. Over the course of a week's time, there was not a single dinner party, not an assembly, not even a picnic, although the weather remained warm and sunny. She enjoyed herself thoroughly.

On the eighth day of her self-enforced exile, she had to admit that all was being done as it should, that her bailiff and staff were keeping everything running as smoothly as if she had never left, and that she had no reason to continue her visit.

Telling herself she would remain a few more days just to rest sounded reasonable. After she had dressed, Annabelle descended to the breakfast room to read the mail and a day-old copy of London's *Post*. The letter from Phoebe revealed that she was much improved, but still bruised enough that she refused to leave the house. Margaret's letter was full of news about the happenings around London, trying, no doubt, to lure Annabelle back to town.

There was a rumble of thunder, and Annabelle looked outside. The beautiful weather they had been enjoying was at an end. She frowned as the rain began to patter against the windows. Sometimes late spring rains made the roads almost impassable.

The day wore on. Luncheon was solitary; no one would venture out to pay calls in this weather. The rain continued, and the wind howled, bending almost double the young saplings at the edge of the garden. Annabelle turned away from the window and pulled a shawl about her shoulders.

She returned to her chair cover. It was the tenth of twelve she was stitching for the breakfast room. Each one was of a bouquet of flowers; this one was roses in all shades of yellow and white. The dim light made it difficult to differentiate between the subtle shades of white, cream, and yellow. She lighted the candles and held it close.

"Blast," she said in disgust and began ripping out the stitching she had done over the past two hours.

The stitching kept her hands busy, but more importantly, it kept her mind occupied. She could spend hours, awake and alert, without thinking of Sir Neville. Or at the very least, giving him only a small portion of her time.

You should thank him for inspiring you to finish these covers, whispered a sardonic voice in her head.

"Not likely," she said aloud, looking around to make certain no one was about to hear her talking to herself. But no, she was alone—completely alone.

She pricked her finger and squeaked in pain. Sucking the drop of blood, she made sure it had quit bleeding before she continued with the cover. It wouldn't do to stain the wool threads with blood.

Annabelle stopped again as the ormolu clock chimed the hour. There, another twenty minutes has passed without thinking of *him!*

The butler entered and said, "My lady, there's some sort of carriage coming up the drive; it's a strange-looking outfit. No top or anything."

Annabelle gladly set aside her needlework and hurried into the hall. The butler threw open the front door, and a footman sped down the steps to grab the horses' heads. The driver jumped to the ground and turned to receive his soaked passenger. They reached the brightness and warmth of the great hall and stopped.

"Good afternoon, Lady Fairfax," said Sinbad Sinclair, his curly brimmed beaver dumping water on the floor as he removed it and bowed.

"Mr. Sinclair!" she exclaimed, stepping forward and unwrapping his bedraggled passenger. "And Charlotte!"

Charlotte burst into tears, hugging Annabelle and sobbing. Annabelle cast a fierce glare at Sinbad, saying to her butler, "See to Mr. Sinclair, Foxton."

"Very good, my lady. If you'll step this way, sir."

Annabelle ushered Charlotte up the stairs to her own room, where a fire already burned in the grate. The sobs were replaced by shivering as the housekeeper and Annabelle dressed Charlotte in a flannel gown and tucked her into the large bed.

After two cups of chocolate laced with brandy, Charlotte's lips had changed back to rosy pink from the ghastly blue they had been upon her arrival. Her shivering ceased, and she nodded sleepily.

"Sleep now, Charlotte. We'll talk later," said Annabelle, blowing out the candles.

Her finger to her lips, she led Mrs. Foxton out of the bedchamber and into the dressing room.

"Come here, my lady. You're almost as wet as the young lady was," said the housekeeper, pulling a coral wool gown out of the armoire. "I know this is a mite heavy, but 'twill feel good for an hour or two."

"I expect you are right," said Annabelle, allowing the motherly housekeeper to unfasten the tiny row of buttons down her back. She discovered she was indeed soaked from handling Charlotte and had to change, as Mrs. Foxton said, "from the skin out." As soon as she was presentable again, she went in search of Sinbad Sinclair.

He presented himself in the morning room wearing strange clothes which fit oddly, his discomfort deriving not only from the embarrassment of his situation but also from the tight fit of his breeches.

"Sit down, Mr. Sinclair," said Annabelle, indicating a chair next to hers.

"I . . . yes, my lady," said the younger man, sitting gingerly on the edge of the chair, his face as pinched as the rest of him.

"What are you doing here with Miss Sweet?"

He blushed scarlet and confessed simply, "We eloped."

"Eloped! Have you lost your mind? Running away with a young lady is inexcusable! What were you thinking? Or were you thinking at all?"

Sinbad loosened the ill-tied cravat at his neck and unfastened the top button of his tight collar.

"I suppose I wasn't thinking too clearly. I missed Charlotte so much; I couldn't think straight."

"That is obvious," said Annabelle indignantly.

"It seemed like such a good idea, like the only idea, when Neville proposed it. I mean, I know he had been having a drink or two, but—"

"He was drunk, you mean. You should have known better than to take advice on such a delicate manner from one such as Sir Neville—be he drunk or stone sober."

"Really, my lady, Neville is the best of fellows," protested Sinbad. "And dash it all, I love her!"

"You have ruined her! How does that show love for her?" came the indefensible question.

Sinbad straightened momentarily before once again slumping down in his confining breeches. "At least, my lady, if I have compromised her, I will now be allowed to wed her."

"Perhaps, Mr. Sinclair, but under such a cloud. Charlotte will be shunned by Society. How will that make her feel?"

Sinbad hung his head and mumbled, "It seemed like such a good idea when we set out this morning."

"This morning?" asked Annabelle, looking thoughtful. "You only left London this morning?"

"Yes," he said, watching with interest as she rose and paced around the room twice before coming back and sitting by his side again.

"Tell me, Mr. Sinclair, what on earth are you doing in Berkshire if you meant to be eloping, I presume, to Gretna Green?"

He blushed again and shifted uncomfortably on the chair. "It started to rain ... Isn't that always the way? We have had a week of warm, sunny days, and then I take her out in Neville's racing curricle—no top, of course—and the rains begin in earnest."

"Back to your story, if you please, sir."

"What? Oh yes, well, I had arranged to pick up Charlotte by the back garden gate at five o'clock in the morning. She was to bring only one small bandbox," he said, adding petulantly, "She had two of the biggest boxes I've ever seen! I managed to hoist one on back and tie it down, but I told her the other would have to be left behind. That started the tears; I should have taken a hint then and there."

"Was my daughter aware of all this?" asked Annabelle sharply.

"Good heavens, no! She would have put a stop to it immediately! No, we decided to keep it between the two of us."

"Go on," said Annabelle, a slight smile curving her lips.

"Anyway, it was almost six o'clock before we got away, but it was only a bit cloudy. We stopped at a small inn outside London to break our fast, and it started to sprinkle. I asked the landlord if there were any back roads that we could take going north that would, you know, parallel the Great North Road; I was afraid we might be followed. He drew me a map, and I swear I followed it precisely, but . . ."

"But you got lost and ended up here," said Annabelle, her smile bright.

"I have a terrible sense of direction," admitted Sinbad sheepishly.

"Your sense of direction may be the only thing that saves all of us from this debacle, Mr. Sinclair. I know you would dearly love to continue your journey northward tomorrow . . ."

Sinbad was already shaking his head, his hands up as though warding off such a suggestion. "Not if it's raining. And not if my Charlotte will be hurt by it, my lady. All I ever wanted was to make her happy."

"Then I have an idea that may save everyone." Recognizing his sudden downcast expression, Annabelle reassured him by saying, "And I think you may even be able to wed Charlotte when all is said and done." Sinbad clasped her hands, his face wreathed in smiles. "If you are very patient," she added.

"Of course, my lady. Anything you say, my lady."

"Very well. First, I will dispatch a letter to Lord Sweet explaining that you and Charlotte arrived on my doorstep early this afternoon."

"Will a messenger be able to get through in this rain?"

"On horseback, certainly. We are not far from the Bath Road; it is always passable. Then tomorrow, we shall all return to London."

"And I shall speak to Lord Sweet."

"And be very, very patient."

"Patient," said Sinbad.

* * *

"Will you be going to the Academy this afternoon, sir?" asked Maltby, retrieving the unread newspaper from its usual spot beside Sir Neville's place in the dining room.

Sir Neville paused at the open door, his hands jammed into the capacious pockets of his dressing gown.

"No, not today." He turned to go.

"Then could you look at the accounts young Mr. Colston sent up from Cornwall, sir? He had one or two questions."

"You take care of it, Maltby."

"I'm not very knowledgeable about agrarian matters, sir."

"Then tell him to do as he pleases with the blasted estate. What do I care?"

Maltby opened his mouth for yet another attempt to interest his master in something; then he shut it and took the chair Sir Neville had lately vacated.

The butler entered and stood quietly, waiting to be addressed.

"What is it, Peters?"

"I thought it best to approach you about the matter first, Mr. Maltby. The head groom has informed me that Mr. Sinclair borrowed Sir Neville's racing curricle last night."

"Racing curricle?" said the puzzled batman. "Oh, that high-perch thing he had a mind to purchase when we came back to England after the war. No matter, Peters. Sir Neville was going to sell it anyway."

"Very good, sir."

The butler turned away, but Maltby asked, "What did Mr. Sinclair want with the thing? He's not enough of a hand to manage it."

"I'm not certain, sir. Shall I ask Plimpton to come to the house?"

"What? No, that's all right. I'll just mention it to Sir Neville; very likely he already knows about it."

The butler inclined his head and left the room. Maltby, still frowning, set aside the newspaper and went in search of Sir Neville.

He found him standing by the window in his studio gazing out at the rain-drenched garden, a canvas in his hands.

"Excuse me, sir."

Neville replaced the canvas on its easel and turned reluctantly toward the voice. His thoughts, filled with painful memories of Annabelle, were troubled, but he left them with regret.

"What is it now, Maltby?"

"Peters just told me that Mr. Sinclair has borrowed your racing curricle."

"My racing curricle? What the devil did he want that for?"

"Peters didn't know, but if you wish, I'll ask Plimpton."

"Don't bother. It doesn't matter. I only hope he will not do himself harm; it's very tricky to drive, even for me."

"Very good, sir," said the batman, turning away.

"When did he borrow it, Maltby?" asked Neville, wiping his hands on a rag.

"Last night, I believe."

"Well, surely he won't attempt to go anywhere in it today. He'll come a cropper for sure," said Neville, frowning.

"He's not as handy with the ribbons as you are, sir."

"No, no he isn't. I think I'll just pop 'round to his

lodgings and see what he's up to. Would you have the carriage brought 'round in half an hour.''

"Gladly, sir," said Maltby, smiling to see the old glint in his master's eye.

An hour later, the entire household was alerted to the fact that Sir Neville was once again his old self. Slamming through the front door as if the wind and rain had propelled him inside, he called for his valet to pack a bag, his pistols to be primed, and his purse to be filled.

"Where are you going?" asked Maltby, even as he hastened to comply with Sir Neville's demands.

Neville, who was halfway to the first landing, spun around and put his finger to his lips. Hurrying back down to his study where Maltby waited, he beckoned Peters to join them.

"A very delicate matter has occurred. I don't want a word of this to get out; a lady's reputation is at stake."

Both men huddled closer while Neville closed the door.

"I am very much afraid that Mr. Sinclair has eloped to Gretna Green with Miss Sweet in my racing curricle."

Chapter Eleven

In less than an hour, Neville and Maltby were ready to leave, their bags already stowed in the boot of the large barouche which rarely saw any action these days.

Stepping into the study, Neville said quietly, "You'll send word if you hear anything, Peters. We'll be taking the Great North Road, making as few stops as necessary."

"Very good, sir," said the butler.

"Excuse me, Mr. Peters," said a footman, standing red-faced in the doorway. "There is a person come to call."

"Then see to it, Donald."

"Begging your pardon, Mr. Peters. It's a young lady, sir," whispered the footman.

"Where is she?" demanded the butler.

"I didn't know what to do with her, sir. I've left her in the hall."

The butler pushed past the footman impatiently. He returned moments later, ushering the caller into Sir

Neville's study. Closing the door behind him, he said quietly, "Miss Fairfax, sir."

"Phoebe! What the devil are you doing here?"

Phoebe's eyes darted between the three men; she licked her lips nervously.

"I need to talk to you, Sir Neville," she whispered. "In private."

"Anything you have to say to me, you can say in front of Maltby and Peters. It will go no further, I promise you."

"It is not that I don't trust you, but it is not my secret to tell," she said, smiling apologetically at the two servants.

"It is Charlotte's," supplied Neville, reaching behind him to pick up his pistols and place them carefully in their case. "And Sinbad's," he added.

"Then you know?" she said, watching him with interest. "You're not going to shoot him, are you? He's your friend!"

"Don't be absurd. The pistols are in case we meet any trouble on the road." At Phoebe's disbelieving stare, he added impatiently, "Highwaymen and such."

"Oh." She frowned suddenly and said, "So the carriage outside is yours. I thought for a moment Charlotte was here. At least I hoped so."

"No, they have actually run away."

"I know that; the silly widgeon left a note for her parents. As if they would have any idea what to say to the Ton! They will probably give it out that she is ill again. Eventually, they will tell everyone she has died rather than face the social and, what's worse, the political scandal."

"So you decided to come here because you wanted a scandal of your own."

"Don't be a gudgeon! Look at me!" she said, dropping her cloak and twirling around.

Maltby's old soul was shocked to see a young lady dressed in breeches and boots, and Peters forgot himself so that he blurted out, "Oh, I say."

Neville leaned back on his desk and grinned. "And what is the purpose of choosing this costume? Going gaming again?"

Phoebe flushed to the color of her hair, and her chin jutted out stubbornly. "As a matter of fact, I came here to enlist your aid in returning Charlotte to her parents before it was too late."

"So, you need my help," he said, smiling.

Phoebe grimaced and said proudly, "As much as it pains me to admit it, yes. I tried renting a carriage and driver by myself, but . . ." She hesitated, not wanting to reveal the humiliating truth. But Sir Neville was waiting and grinning in the most infuriating manner, and Phoebe plunged ahead. "I tried two different posting inns and neither would rent to me—either as a female or a male."

"Oho! So you mean to go with me?"

"That is what I planned."

"Well, let me disabuse you of any such notion, my girl. I'm not about to take you along to be compromised, too."

"You can't compromise a boy!" she said, striding manfully up to Sir Neville and glaring at him, her nose almost reaching his chin. "Besides, how do you think it will look if you do find them? How can Charlotte's reputation be saved by traveling with two men who are not her relatives?"

Neville refused to acknowledge the logic of this, but Maltby said, "She has a point there, sir."

"Shaddup," he snapped, peering down his nose at

her now-smug expression. "What about the Sweets? How will you explain your absence?"

Phoebe grinned, looking like the cat that swallowed the cream. "When I found Charlotte's note, I took it and substituted one of my own."

"Which said?"

"It said that my mother had sent for me, so Charlotte and I were going for a short visit in the country to revive her spirits. She has been so glum, they will believe it."

"It might work," said Neville.

"I must protest, sir. You can't mean to be taking the young lady," said Peters.

Neville heaved a sigh of resignation. "Bested by a slip of a girl, Maltby. It's not like the army," he said, his eyes shining with amusement. "Come on, brat. We're wasting time. By the way, this is Maltby—Mr. Maltby to you; do everything he tells you to. He has more sense than the both of us put together."

"Pay him no heed, miss," said Maltby, standing aside for Phoebe to pass first.

Neville led the way to the carriage, helping Phoebe pull the huge greatcoat around her face and patting her hat down farther on her head.

"Not there, infant. You may sit in the rear-facing seat."

"No, sir, let the child sit by you," said Maltby.

"Nonsense! She wanted to come along; she'll sit where I tell her to. Besides, she's young, and you're not. Neither am I, for that matter. She should want to sit there, out of respect for her elders."

When Phoebe was safely inside, on the rear-facing seat, she stuck out her tongue at Sir Neville and favored Maltby with a sweet smile.

"Truly, sir, I don't mind. I can ride just any which way," said Phoebe.

"If you're sure, miss," said the batman, already well on the way to being won over by their charge.

"I'm positive," said Phoebe, earning a nod of thanks from Neville.

Maltby climbed back into the carriage and shook his head. "I'm sorry, major, sir. The landlord said no one has come by all day in a high perch phaeton."

"Then they must have turned off," said Sir Neville, his long fingers drumming an impatient tattoo on the seat beside him. "They must have stopped at that little inn in the last village. I should have known he would be avoiding the larger posting inns. Turn 'em around, Antonio!"

"It's getting late, sir. I don't see how we'll find them if they've left the main road," said Maltby.

"Have a bit of faith, Maltby. If there is one person whose strategy I know, it's Sinclair. If he's not left England, I'll find him. What say you, Phoebe, do we continue on?"

Phoebe stretched her aching muscles and nodded. "We have no choice. And it can't be past five o'clock."

Neville held out his watch. "More like six, but we are making progress, I think."

Antonio, who was loving every minute of driving the traveling carriage, even in the rain, called a loud halloo to the inn when they arrived. The door opened, and the innkeeper himself trudged outside, an oiled slicker over his head.

"What can I do for you, sir?" he asked.

"Have you seen a high perch phaeton today?"

"Aye, sir, this morning it was. Friends of yours?"

"Stay here, Phoebe," whispered Neville before he hopped to the ground and hurried into the inn, Maltby on his heels. Shaking the rain from his greatcoat, he asked, "Which way were they headed when they left here?"

The innkeeper rubbed his hands together and said slyly, "You wouldn't be the young lady's father or uncle or anything?"

Neville picked the man up by his collar, giving him a little shake. "Which way did they go?" he growled.

The innkeeper pried Sir Neville's fingers off and smiled nervously. "I was just curious like, sir. I meant no harm. I see a lot of 'em, those swell toffs with their little ladies scared out o' their wits."

"And you saw the one today driving the phaeton?"

"Aye, and the little lady half sick with cold and damp. But they were set on going on, don't you see. So they asked me fer directions, to th' back roads, don't you see, so anyone following 'em won't be able t' find 'em."

"And you gave them such directions?"

"Aye," said the landlord, smiling widely. "I allays does. I gives 'em directions so they'll end up right back where they started, or so close to it as to make no difference."

Neville took a step back and looked at Maltby, a slight smile curving his lips for the first time that day. Maltby grinned.

"You mean you make a habit of misdirecting couples who are trying to elope?"

"It's just a little service I like t' perform, sir. I have three daughters of me own; I can understand a father's concern," said the landlord piously.

Sir Neville nodded knowingly and took out his purse. "And the fathers come across with a handsome reward."

"Only what they feel the service is worth, sir. Oh, thank you, sir. If you like, I can give you the same directions so you can follow after them. I can tell you,

I wasn't too impressed with that young man's driving ability. He nearly turned the thing over in my yard!''

"He can be rather ham-fisted. And yes, I think we should have those directions. What might they cost?'' asked Neville.

The landlord put out his hand and said magnanimously, "Not a penny, sir, not a penny. It's my pleasure; that it is. You see, first you take the next road to your left, just past the next farmhouse. You go along that road for, oh, a quarter of an hour, until you reach a crossroads Go slow, or you'll miss it. Next . . .''

An hour later, any hint of a smile was long forgotten.

"Bloody hell! I'm going to kill that Sinclair when we do catch up with him,'' swore Neville, panting heavily before starting to push the back of the carriage once again. It was mired up to the axles in sucking mud. Antonio called to the horses and applied the whip, and Neville and Maltby put their shoulders to the wheels again.

"Promise you'll let me help,'' grumbled Maltby.

"Not if I get to him first. I'm going to choke the life out of him.''

"Let me help push,'' said Phoebe, moving to the side of the carriage and taking hold.

"Stay out of the way, Phoebe. We'll manage.''

"I'm very strong,'' she said.

"And I'm very angry right now. Just do as you're told,'' snapped Sir Neville.

Even in the rain, with her coat soaked and her hat melting onto her head, she managed to flounce away from the carriage. Ignoring her, the men continued to rock the carriage back and forth.

"It's no use,'' said Neville. "I'll walk to the next village and see if I can hire a vehicle.''

"Let me, sir,'' said Maltby.

"No, you stay here with Miss Fairfax and see she comes to no harm—from villains or herself!"

Phoebe tossed her head to show what she thought of his comments.

"How far do you think you'll have to walk?"

"According to our innkeeper, the village of Pangbourne shouldn't be too much—"

"Pangbourne?" said Phoebe, joining them again. "But Pangbourne is just east of my home!"

"Are you sure, miss?" asked Maltby.

"Of course I am," she began confidently. Then she added, "Unless there could be another village called Pangbourne?"

"There's only one I know," said Sir Neville. "You know, Maltby, I think our little fox has gone to ground."

"It is possible, sir, with the weather and all."

"Phoebe, would Charlotte recognize the town of Pangbourne? I mean, would she know you live close by it?"

"Of course. Not only has she visited me often, but we would always go to Pangbourne on market day," she said, her excitement growing. "Do you think it is possible they have gone to Fairbridge?"

"If Fairbridge is your estate, I think it highly likely. Sinclair wouldn't risk travel at night, in the rain, on unfamiliar roads. They must be there," said Sir Neville, feeling a lightness in his heart. "Lead on, my girl, lead on."

Annabelle took her place at the dining table, Sinbad on her right and a much brighter Charlotte on her left. Except for an occasional comment on the weather, they kept silent as one course after another was served.

When Annabelle rose to signal the end of the meal,

she said, "Foxton, please bring Mr. Sinclair's port to the drawing room. We don't mind his joining us there."

"Very good, my lady," said the butler, never raising an eyebrow.

When they were finally alone, Annabelle looked at her two runaways and shook her head. Charlotte wore one of Annabelle's gowns, her portmanteau and everything in it having been soaked. The gown was six or seven inches too short, and Charlotte's stocking feet—too large to fit into borrowed shoes—were exposed. Sinclair had happily changed out of his borrowed clothes and now wore his own breeches and shirt, which had been dried by the kitchen fire; his coat was still too damp.

They were a pitiful sight, but watching their joy at being together again was like attending a display of fireworks. Their glances sparkled, bursting into flames when their eyes met. One could almost feel their love, thought Annabelle. The realization that they had come through this terrible ordeal more in love than ever filled her with awe and melancholy.

If only she and Neville . . . But no, one had to be in love first, before adversity could strengthen that love. And he, at least, had never been in love.

"My lady," said Charlotte, tearing her eyes away from Sinbad. "You are planning to return to London with us tomorrow, are you not?"

"Of course. I wouldn't let you face your mother alone. She is a very dear person, but I fear she will be very angry," said Annabelle.

"I shall be there, too, my love," said Sinbad, taking Charlotte's hand in his.

Annabelle turned away from their soulful gazes; she tried not to remember when Neville had gazed at her just so. Except, she reminded herself, his regard had been a lie.

She had gone over it again and again. She thought she had gotten past the self-recrimination and interrogation. But seeing the young lovers had reawakened all the heartbreak and confusion. Had he only been doing as he told Phoebe—helping to find someone else to be her husband? Or had he been engaging in a passionate flirtation? Or had he been making game of her?

"My lady? Are you all right?" asked Sinclair.

"What? Yes, I'm fine. I think we should make an early night of it. Charlotte?" she said, rising and walking to the door.

Charlotte and Sinbad rose also, but Charlotte made no effort to join Annabelle. Her eyes were locked on Sinbad's as though she were bewitched.

That is what love is supposed to be like, thought Annabelle, not some passionate assignation in a broom closet or on a terrace. Love was made up of feelings from deep in the heart.

Annabelle announced loudly, "I'll just go up and make sure the maid has laid out Phoebe's nightrail for you, Charlotte. I'll expect you in a moment or two."

Annabelle trudged up the stairs, wishing she could feel happiness for the couple. Instead, witnessing their infatuation with each other was like pouring salt in an open wound. Her pain was renewed in full force. She wiped her eyes angrily.

After fifteen minutes, and still no Charlotte, Annabelle blew her nose and dried her damp eyes. Shaking her head, she started back down to the drawing room. As she reached the first landing, the front door crashed open, and three drenched figures burst into the great hall.

"What is the meaning . . ." began the butler, two

footmen seconding him as he approached the intruders. The smallest removed her hat, and Foxton exclaimed, "Miss Phoebe! Why I . . . Come in, miss, come in!"

He helped remove her coat, and she stretched like a cat, moving toward the warmth of the fire.

Glancing at the staircase, Phoebe cried, "Mother!" and rushed up the stairs to be caught in her mother's embrace.

"What in the world are you doing here? And who . . ."

Phoebe stepped back and watched the blood drain from her mother's cheeks.

"You," she whispered before slipping to the floor.

"Mother! Mother!"

"Annabelle," breathed Neville, rushing to her side.

Sinbad and Charlotte also rushed to the aid of their hostess.

"Get back," said Maltby. "All of you step aside. She needs air, not smothering."

"You heard him," barked Neville.

"You, too, sir," said the batman. Sir Neville backed away. Maltby opened the bag he always carried and took out some smelling salts. A quick wave under her nose reanimated Annabelle; coughing, she struggled to sit up. "Easy, my lady. Take it very slowly."

"Move, Maltby, and I'll take her upstairs," said Neville, coming forward and reaching for Annabelle.

"No! Stay away from me!"

"Nonsense, I'm just going to carry you to your room, Annabelle," said Neville, frowning fiercely.

"Don't touch me," she whispered, her voice cracking and tears starting to her eyes.

"Allow me, sir. Her ladyship is not herself," said Maltby.

"Oh, but I think she is," said Neville quietly as he moved away, his eyes shuttered.

Maltby bent back down, and Annabelle asked weakly, "Who are you?"

"Maltby, my lady, at your service." He looked up and motioned the butler forward. "If you'll take her other arm, sir, we can get her upstairs."

"I'm sure I can walk," said Annabelle, feeling gingerly of the lump on the side of her head.

They ignored her and practically carried her up the stairs to her room. Phoebe followed, but the others remained frozen in place.

When Annabelle was safe in bed, she looked at her daughter and shook her head. "Up to your old tricks?"

"Not tricks, Mother. I have saved the day, as they say."

"And how have you done that, young lady, traipsing all over the countryside with two strange men."

"Sir Neville is hardly a stranger to you," teased Phoebe without realizing the pain her words caused. "And the one who helped you to bed was Mr. Maltby. He is Sir Neville's batman, or he was during the war. We have come to rescue Charlotte."

"Rescue Charlotte? I hardly think that necessary since she has been with me for most of the day," said Annabelle, leaning back against the pillows and closing her eyes again.

"Mother, I am not a child. I found Charlotte's note; I know what she was trying to do. But never fear, I tore up that note and left a different one saying she and I were coming here to visit you. I had no idea we would actually end up here, but that's all to the better!"

"There is only one problem with your plan, Phoebe. I sent a messenger to Margaret earlier to inform her that Charlotte was safe with me."

"Oh, no, Mother!"

"Yes, so you see, all your efforts have gone for naught.

"I'm sorry, Mother," she said in a small voice.

"Phoebe, I'm really too tired to discuss it tonight. You and Charlotte may share your room; we leave for London first thing in the morning."

"Good, we can use Sir Neville's carriage."

"We will not," said Annabelle firmly, her head beginning to ache. "And I'll not hear another word about the man. I'll provide him shelter for tonight, but I do not want to see him. You may tell him he's to keep to his room until we are gone tomorrow."

"Mother!"

"Tell him," said Annabelle, her brow rising ominously.

"Yes, ma'am," said Phoebe. Muttering, she left the room and made her way back downstairs. She paused to give Foxton instructions about the extra guests before approaching Sir Neville.

"How is she?" he asked anxiously.

"She will be fine, I think."

"I want to see her."

"She is probably asleep by now," lied Phoebe.

"Surely not yet." Neville studied her pink cheeks and said, "She doesn't want to see me?"

"No," whispered Phoebe.

"What did she say?"

"She . . . she said she would provide a room for you, but she wanted you to stay in it until after we have left for London on the morrow."

Neville's jaw clenched, and he shook his head slowly. "Maltby!" he roared.

"Yes sir?"

"Have the carriage brought around again. We're going to an inn for the night."

"But sir—"

"Sir Neville, no! You mustn't!" cried Phoebe and Charlotte.

"Not good form," said Sinbad, placing his hand on Neville's sleeve to restrain him.

Neville turned, the coldness in his gray eyes causing everyone to step back."To hell with 'good form,' and to hell with you—all of you!"

Chapter Twelve

When Annabelle awoke the next morning, it was just past daybreak. She rubbed her eyes and pulled herself up on the pillows, wishing she could pull the covers back over her head and block out the light and her thoughts.

She had behaved very badly, she knew. But it had been such a shock to see him there, in her home, her sanctuary. He had been filthy, his greatcoat covered in mud. When he removed his coat, she could see he was soaked to the skin, his smooth jaw shadowed by a dark stubble, and his eyes filled with concern for her.

Concern? Hah! He had invaded her home just as he constantly invaded her thoughts and dreams. She had thought she was well on the way to—not forgetting, but at least forgiving herself for her folly. But she had only been fooling herself. Fooling the fool! she reflected bitterly.

And now she was going back to London. It would be

impossible to avoid seeing him, to avoid hearing about him. Would this nightmare never end?

Sir Neville tried to stretch his legs and hit the foot rail. He turned on his side and almost fell off the bed.

Catching himself, he muttered curses under his breath and crawled off the narrow cot. His hands in the small of his back, he stretched and groaned. A violent sneeze bent him over, and he muttered a sarcastic thanks to Annabelle for the bout of pneumonia he was probably developing.

So much for his indignant flight from her, he thought. When he had stormed out of the house, the steady rain of the day had turned suddenly brutal, frightening the young Antonio so, he had been incapable of driving the carriage. Cursing everything and everyone, Neville had taken over the box, his way lighted by the bolts of lightning flashing through the heavens.

The only inn in Pangbourne was filled to the gills with other rain-weary travelers. The landlord had finally offered to oust his son from his truckle bed and move it into the private parlor for Sir Neville. Maltby slept on the hard floor, a blanket wrapped around him.

Neville sneezed again and blew his nose.

As he moved stiffly around the room, Maltby stopped snoring and opened his eyes. "Sleep well, sir?"

"I should have followed your example. It couldn't have been any worse than those cursed huts in Spain," said Neville.

"A little better, really. Those floors were never even. This one is just as hard, but at least it's level. How was the truckle bed?"

"About two feet too short and three too narrow," said Neville. He added two logs and stirred up the fire;

then he held out his hands to the meager flames. Glancing at Maltby, Neville grimaced. "I know what you're thinking, but I wasn't about to remain in that dashed house another minute."

"Very good, sir," said Maltby, rising with some difficulty.

Neville said grudgingly, "Suppose I should have considered your opinion." Maltby only grunted, and Neville added waspishly, "I know you're not as young as you once were. I wager your old bones will be stiff for a week."

"No stiffer than yours . . . sir."

There was a scratching at the door; Neville bit off the scathing retort he had been about to utter and crossed the room to open the door. Phoebe stumbled into the parlor, and he steadied her with a quick hand.

"That's what happens to young ladies who listen at keyholes," said Neville, leaving the door open and returning to the hearth, carefully choosing the most comfortable chair.

"I was not listening," said Phoebe, very much on her dignity. Then she spoiled her act by grinning and saying, "I was peeking inside to see if you were awake yet."

"Glad I wasn't busy raping and pillaging," said Neville.

"As if you would," said Phoebe, walking toward his chair and sinking down on the stool in front of him. She wore a dark green cloak against the morning chill and a serviceable bonnet. There was no hint of the ragamuffin lad from the day before; she was every inch the lady.

Neville thought idly that he preferred her with a smudged face and breeches. Softening his tone, he asked, "So what brings you here, brat? Another damsel-in-distress tale?"

"No, not at all. I just wanted to thank you for what you did yesterday. I know it turned out fine—for Charlotte and Mr. Sinclair, that is. But afterward, well . . . . I'm sorry about all that."

"Think nothing of it. I'm sure I shan't. Now, will you stay to break your fast with us?"

Impetuously, Phoebe took his large hands in hers and lifted them to her lips. With a catch in her voice she said, "No, I must return quickly. Mother . . . that is, we wish to be away by ten o'clock. Thank you again, Sir Neville. And you, too, Mr. Maltby. I couldn't have managed without you. Goodbye."

"Goodbye, brat," said Neville, allowing Maltby to see her outside to the pony cart.

Neville moved to the window to watch her departure. Phoebe had somehow wormed her way into his heart. Her mother was a . . .

Shaking his head, Neville returned to the fire. Annabelle. How had she become so important to him? For the first time, he faced the fact that he had lost her. And forgetting her was no longer a matter of simply avoiding her; she was with him every waking moment— and usually in his dreams, too.

The fire, which had been so warm and inviting, was suddenly too hot. Angry tears started to his eyes, and he threw himself out of the chair and charged out of the room, hurrying through the kitchens and startling the landlord and his family.

After a brisk walk through the woods behind the inn, Neville found the peace he sought. While he had never been in love before, as a soldier, he had engaged in many battles on the Peninsula. At times, the odds against them had seemed insurmountable. But at Talavera and Corunna, Neville recalled, despite being outnumbered, they had won the day. And at Salamanca, Wellington had confounded the enemy, changing directions and snatching victory out of a near defeat.

Perhaps, thought Neville, I have been too complacent in my courtship. Simply deciding I want to have Annabelle for my wife is obviously not sufficient to win her. It will require strategy, perhaps even a siege.

A wicked smile curving his lips, Neville returned to the inn, requesting a hearty breakfast before they began their journey.

"Here it is, my lady!" exclaimed Charlotte, thrusting the *Morning Post* at Annabelle and Phoebe.

One week after their return to London, the ladies were gathered in the drawing room, all dressed in quiet elegance, waiting for the first of the visitors which the announcement in the newspaper would inevitably bring. Charlotte was one of the first young ladies of the Season to be betrothed, and while it was not a brilliant match, it was certainly respectable.

"Now it is official," said Phoebe, managing a smile.

Annabelle gave her a nod of approval, knowing how hard it was for Phoebe to be happy about this—or any match. Phoebe had confided in her only the night before that she was torn between joy for her friend and sadness at losing the Charlotte who was always willing to share her escapades. Now, Phoebe realized it could never be the same.

Annabelle glanced at the announcement and said, "Best wishes, my dear. I hope you will be very happy," leaning over to kiss Charlotte's flushed cheek.

"I only wish Mama—"

"She will come about, especially after this afternoon. I feel certain we will be inundated with well-wishers. Sinbad will be here, of course, and the two of you will bask in all the congratulatory messages. That will surely soften your mother's censure," said Annabelle.

"I hope you may be right, my lady," said Charlotte.

Phoebe read the announcement again and grinned. "You know that any remaining reservations she may have will disappear next year when the announcement is about the birth of her first grandchild."

Charlotte blushed a deep rose color, and Annabelle, though smiling too, said, "Phoebe! Must you be so unrefined?"

"I see you are all here," announced Lady Margaret Sweet, fixing her daughter with a cool stare as she and Charlotte's father entered the room.

"Yes, Mama," murmured Charlotte, brightening as her father winked at her.

"You may as well speak up, Charlotte. You're going to be a married woman in a very short time. You must learn to deal with all sorts of people."

"I'm certain Charlotte will deal admirably," said Lord Sweet, favoring his wife with a warning glance. "I wish I could stay for the mass of visitors you will no doubt have, my dear, but duty calls."

"Goodbye, Papa."

Annabelle reflected that Margaret was too accustomed to ordering her life and the lives of those around her to accept easily any arrangements made without her guiding hand. But she would recover. And Annabelle vowed to do all she could to help smooth Charlotte's path; both mother and daughter would be glad of her help in the end.

Still waiting for their first callers, Annabelle said, "Have you decided which of the modistes will have the privilege of making your wedding gown, Charlotte?"

"I haven't considered," she replied, jumping as Phoebe pinched the back of her hand and nodded toward Lady Sweet. "That is, who do you think we should go to, Mama?"

"Madam Lemieux, of course. She designed the gown for the Hadley girl last year. It was beautiful, and very different. We must consult with her tomorrow."

"What a good idea," said Phoebe.

Annabelle threw her a warning look, but Lady Sweet was only warming up and hadn't caught the obvious flattery.

"For the rest of the bride clothes, we should visit other modistes as well. After all, my dear, you don't want all your gowns to look alike."

"I suppose not," said Charlotte, her eyes wide with surprise.

"Sir Neville Colston and Mr. Sinclair," intoned the butler. Annabelle jumped, her eyes darting this way and that, looking for an escape.

Sinbad, very conscious of still being in Lady Sweet's black books, bowed deeply to his future mother-in-law and then to Annabelle. Next, he turned to the young ladies, taking a chair opposite the sofa where they perched.

Sir Neville was just as much on his dignity, but his bow before Annabelle was perfunctory. He ignored the empty chair by her side and pulled up another close to Phoebe.

"How are you today, Sir Neville?" she asked.

"Quite well, Miss Fairfax. And you?"

"I am fine," said Phoebe, uncertain how to proceed.

Thus ignored, Annabelle surreptitiously pinched her cheeks, which she felt certain had blanched upon Sir Neville's entrance. Her heartbeat was doing strange things, and she concentrated on breathing evenly.

"What do you think, Annabelle?" Lady Sweet was

saying. "Could we not pull together and throw a ball, an engagement ball, in two weeks' time?"

"Two weeks?" said Annabelle, careful to keep her gaze on Margaret only. "I think you and I are capable of organizing an absolutely marvelous engagement ball."

Glad to have a safe topic of conversation, Annabelle favored her audience with a smile. Then her face fell as Sir Neville spoke again.

"You'll save me a waltz, Miss Fairfax? And you, Miss Sweet, a quadrille?" Staring pointedly at Annabelle, he added, "You notice, I don't ask for a boulanger; when it is performed, I much prefer a quiet . . . conversation on the balcony."

Annabelle turned scarlet, remembering well the events leading up to their first kiss. But Sir Neville appeared unaware of her discomfort. With a warm smile for the rest of his audience, the man excused himself, claiming another appointment.

Annabelle felt she would swoon. Such a silly thing, she chided herself, but her color must have changed drastically because even Mr. Sinclair noticed and poured her a glass of sherry.

The interminable afternoon dragged on. Annabelle knew Sir Neville would not return, but every time the drawing room door opened, she looked up, alarmed.

What is he up to now? she asked herself a hundred times over. He had not addressed himself to her. Neither had he appeared uncomfortable being in her presence.

The dismal thought occurred to Annabelle that Sir Neville, never having been in love with her in the first place, felt no sense of embarrassment to be in her company now. She wished she could feel the same, but a deep feeling of shame at her gullibility prevented it. Annabelle, who had always been in complete control, had to admit that Sir Neville Colston caused her world to tilt crazily on its axis, turning everything upside-down and wrong-side-out.

And Sir Neville was to be Mr. Sinclair's best man for the upcoming nuptials, she thought, cringing. For the next month, they were likely to meet frequently.

Then so be it, resolved Annabelle; if he can meet with equanimity, then so can I!

Sir Neville's fist came crashing down on the invitation, causing the papers on his desk to jump in fright. Two weeks he had spent, seeing Annabelle in the park, at the theater, at Lady Sweet's town house; two weeks without a single personal comment addressed to her.

Oh, she was becoming more accustomed to his presence; her porcelain complexion no longer turned red or white when he entered the room. In fact, she was able to address innocuous comments somewhere over his shoulder without a single stammer. In short, thought Neville angrily, he did not affect her at all.

Sir Neville was dressed in coal black with only his white cravat to relieve the severity of his dress. Even the jewel in his cravat was black onyx; it glittered like his dangerous eyes.

Maltby, who had heard the boom of his fist, opened the study door charily.

"What do you want?" growled Sir Neville.

"Your carriage is at the door, sir. I know you prefer the curricle, but it's beginning to rain, so I told—"

"That's fine, just fine," said Neville, rubbing his sore fist gingerly. "Tell them not to wait up for me. I may not come back until tomorrow."

"Yes, sir."

Sir Neville left the room, pausing impatiently to allow Peters to place his greatcoat around his shoulders.

The short ride to the Sweets' town house did not improve Neville's temper. He had promised himself that he would be the perfect, insipid gentleman with Annabelle. Starting out fresh with her was his only chance, so he had told himself. But his strategy wasn't working. She showed no sign of allowing herself to relax with him, much less to welcome his advances.

Tonight, he would put it to the test. He would take her onto the . . . No, not the balcony; their encounters outside had led only to heartbreak and frustration. He would get her alone somehow, and he would ask her to marry him. It was as simple as that.

So what will you do if she rejects you? he asked his reflection in the window of the carriage. His fists clenched involuntarily. He wouldn't worry about that now. She simply must accept him!

Annabelle remained seated at the dressing table, her eyes never leaving her image, but never seeing it either. She was beyond tears. Those were spent each night before sleep and exhaustion finally overtook her.

"My lady?" said Mary quietly. "It's time to be going down to dinner, my lady."

"What? Oh, of course. Thank you, Mary, you've done an admirable job," said Annabelle automatically.

The maid curtseyed and left the room. Annabelle smoothed the watered silk and put her hand to her throat where a single ruby was suspended by a heavy gold chain. Her garnet ball gown, ordered new for this engagement celebration, didn't fit right. She had had little appetite since returning to London, and had lost weight. The modiste had been too busy to make the last-minute alterations, and Annabelle hadn't cared.

Seeing her reflection, she reached for a rouge pot

and applied a little color to her cheeks. She grimaced; it only accentuated the dark circles under her eyes.

He would be there, probably already was. Being best man, he had been invited to dinner, of course. After the bride and groom began the first waltz, he would lead Phoebe onto the floor. His tall, graceful form would make Phoebe appear a mere child. He would be wearing black, perhaps with a waistcoat of silver to match his eyes. That was the way she would always remember him—the way he had dressed when they were waltzing at Almack's.

Tears welled up in her eyes, and Annabelle dabbed at them gently.

"Now then, no more of that, my girl," she told her image stoutly. "Tonight is Charlotte's special night; nothing shall spoil it."

Besides, she told herself, she had sworn not to allow Sir Neville Colston to get the best of her. Let him think she had no feelings toward him at all. That was the way to regain her self-respect. She couldn't expect revenge, of course.

Her eyes in the mirror narrowed thoughtfully. What if she could get some sort of revenge on him? Would it make her feel better? Would it allow her some peace of mind? Seeking revenge was supposed to be bad for one, but when she tried on the thought, it didn't *feel* bad. It felt wonderful, she thought, smiling at her image for the first time. Revenge—it was something to consider. But how?

"Annabelle? Are you ready? The dinner guests are arriving. We must hurry," called Margaret.

"Coming," she said, making her way to the door.

The good thing about helping Margaret organize the dinner party before the ball, reflected Annabelle as she

sat down at the long mahogany table, was that she had
arranged to be placed on the same side of the table as
her nemesis and as far away as possible. She could neither see him nor hear his voice. She heard Phoebe from
time to time, and Phoebe was his partner, but he kept
his voice low.

No matter how hard she strained her ears, she
couldn't hear him. No matter how far forward she
leaned, she couldn't see him. Fortunately, the irony of
these thoughts was lost on Annabelle.

When she had gone downstairs, her eyes had been
drawn to him like a magnet the moment she entered
the drawing room where their guests were gathered.
He had been in conversation with Phoebe, his eyes
teasing her as he leaned down to whisper something.
Phoebe had laughed aloud, her face full of mischief.
But Annabelle's gaze had alerted him to her presence,
it seemed, for he had turned and inclined his head to
her. She had responded, she thought, but she wasn't
sure. With a word to Phoebe, he had started toward her,
but she had been saved by the butler calling everyone to
the dining room.

Now, having reassured herself she would not be bothered by him, Annabelle turned with relief as Lord West
claimed her attention. He was a true gentleman; if he
was disappointed to find himself partnering the mother
instead of her daughter, his manners were too well
honed for him to show it.

"Have you decided to accompany us to Vauxhall
tomorrow night, my lady?" he asked.

"Yes, I think I should go. It is very nice of your mother
to include all of us in her party."

"Well, she's got m' sister to launch next fall, during
the Little Season. She lives in the country most of the

time, too, so she thought it a good idea to come up for a week or two to renew acquaintances."

"That's very true, and I'm sure Lady Sweet will be delighted to help next fall. She plans to present Charlotte's twin sisters, you know."

"Twins?"

"Caroline and Annabelle."

"Oh, I say, the second one's named for you, eh?"

"Precisely," said Annabelle, smiling. She understood perfectly Phoebe's fondness for Lord West; he was such a pleasant young man.

"I shall be sure to tell Mother about them. If Susan can meet them immediately when she comes to town, she won't be so shy. It's dashed difficult for me to be any help. Half the fellows I know, well, a man doesn't necessarily think his friends meet the expectations he has for his sister."

"I think your feelings do you credit, Lord West. I often wished I had a brother to look after my interests." Lord West pinked up and shook his head in protest.

Margaret rose, signaling to the ladies that it was time to leave the gentlemen to their port. Instead of gathering in the drawing room, the ladies separated to repair their hair before the remainder of the guests began arriving for the ball. Annabelle slipped away to the kitchen for a quick consult with Cook before taking the back stairs to her room.

She removed her gloves and patted her hair, noticing the pins were coming out in one spot. She had only been inside a moment when there was a quiet knock on the door. Thinking it was one of the girls, she continued brushing an escaped curl of hair and bade her visitor enter.

"Annabelle," said Neville, struck afresh by her beauty. The brush clattered as it fell onto the marble top of the dressing table. Her heart did a flip, and she froze, not daring to move, hoping her beleaguered mind was only playing a lascivious trick on her.

"Annabelle."

It was no trick, and she turned to face him. Her legs were suddenly unable to support her, and she sat down suddenly on the bench behind her. Damn him, she thought. Neville strode across the room and knelt before her, taking her hands in his and kissing them tenderly.

Annabelle withdrew them, noticing in confusion that they were shaking uncontrollably. But Neville captured them again.

"Annabelle, my dearest, I had forgotten how very green your eyes are. You are so beautiful," he said, lifting her hands to his lips. She shook her head and tried to pull away, but his hands gently imprisoned hers.

Annabelle bowed her head, refusing to meet his eyes. Why was he doing this to her? Didn't he realize she didn't want to listen to his empty compliments, that she couldn't participate in such a shallow flirtation—not even if she weren't so painfully in love with him.

But he either couldn't see how his seductive words wounded her, or he simply didn't care.

"Don't you know how I feel about you? Every time I see you, I want to take you in my arms, Annabelle. Please, you must listen to me."

She raised her head, her chin tilted proudly, her eyes free of tears.

He leaned forward and captured her lips for a brief kiss before saying hoarsely, "Will you marry me?"

"Marry?" she whispered, joy replacing her confusion. Neville nodded hopefully.

"Marry?" she repeated, her voice stronger than

before as her fears and doubts replaced the fleeting joy she had felt seconds before.

He couldn't be serious! How many times had they been in each other's company in the past two weeks, and never had he even hinted at feelings of warmth for her. And now this? What part could this charade play in his flirtation? Was this only another ploy to get her into his bed? Did he expect her to fall at his feet, grateful for this crumb of decency before seducing her?

Playing for time as her anger grew, Annabelle rose, and Neville released her hands, rising also. "Marry you?" she said slowly.

Annabelle moved to the window and stared outside a moment. The room overlooked the small garden which was to have been lighted with an array of colorful lanterns, but the rain had precluded those plans.

The darkness outside comforted Annabelle; she gathered strength from it, the strength to do whatever it might take to regain her peace of mind, to rid herself of this obsession for Neville Colston. She turned to face him again, her eyes cold and unfeeling.

"You want me to say I will marry you? Are you certain you know what you are asking? You see, I believe marriage is forever. And a marriage without love, well, it is not to be considered. So, Sir Neville, do you mean to say you love me?"

Neville frowned. This was not going as planned. He would not have been surprised had she simply turned him down. But this interrogation . . . He didn't know if it boded well or ill.

Ignoring the voice in his mind which urged caution, Neville smiled at her and said, "Perhaps I should show you how I feel."

He crossed the room and would have taken her in his arms, if Annabelle had allowed it. But she held him at arms' length, her mind replaying his words. Why hadn't he simply confessed his love for her? cried her heart. Ruthlessly, Annabelle silenced the voice. He hadn't said he loved her, so that was that. No, he only wanted her. Whatever he felt for her was not strong enough to be labeled as love. Still he persisted in this sham, asking her to wed when he felt nothing for her but lust, knowing he could not possess her body without marriage.

At that moment, Annabelle came very close to hating him. Suddenly, the desire to hurt him was overwhelming. I'll agree she thought. I'll agree to marry him and then tell him I'm not going to, that I simply can't, that I . . . don't love him.

Ruthlessly, her heart shouted down the cry of indignation at such an untruth. But her mind was in control now, and the desire for recompense was almost heady.

But Neville was frowning down at her and asking again, "So, will you do me the honor of being my wife?"

"Yes, Sir Neville, I believe I will."

Chapter Thirteen

Neville enfolded Annabelle in a tender embrace. He lifted her chin and kissed her, his lips requiring her cooperation which she allowed herself to give, returning his kisses with genuine enthusiasm, telling herself—while her mind was still active—that her surrender now would only add to his pain when she denounced him and their counterfeit betrothal in a few moments—a few breathless moments. And she surrendered to his kisses.

Neville swung her into his arms and moved to the bed, where he cradled her, kissing her lips, her ear, her neck. Annabelle arched against him, and he cupped her full breast, his lips trailing fire across the exposed skin. She grasped his hair and moaned, all her anguish washed away by wave after wave of desire.

"Mother' " called Phoebe, alerting them to her imminent entrance.

Neville slipped off the bed, moving to a chair by the fire, smoothing his dark hair and crossing his legs uncomfortably. Annabelle pulled her gown into shape and was sitting primly on the side of the bed when Phoebe stepped into the room.

"Mother, my pearls have broken. Do you have anything suitable for me to . . . Oh," said Phoebe, her eyes growing wide when she spied Neville.

"Let us see what we can find," said Annabelle, willing her heart to stop pounding and her hands to steady as she crossed the room to her dressing table and began rummaging through her jewel case.

"Hello again, Phoebe," said Neville, trying not to blush or grin stupidly.

"Sir Neville," she said, inclining her head slightly. Most young women would have left it at that, good manners commanding that their curiosity be stifled, but Phoebe was not like *most* young women. "What are you doing in here?" she demanded, more puzzled than angry.

"I desired a word in private with your mother, so I followed her up here," said Neville, knowing that Phoebe would not be satisfied with such a singularly uninformative explanation, but waiting for Annabelle to inform her daughter of their impending marriage.

"Mother?"

Annabelle ceased her search through her jewelry case and turned, facing her daughter first and then Neville— her betrothed, she thought miserably. What had she been thinking? She must tell him at once! If their betrothal became public, she would be honor-bound to go through with the marriage, and while her heart wanted nothing more than to be his wife, she could not accept his terms. She couldn't be satisfied with a loveless marriage. What would become of her after their shared lust was satisfied? What would be left for her then?

But Sir Neville, who gave all the appearance of a man

delirious with happiness, announced suddenly, "Phoebe, you must wish us happy. Your mother has agreed to be my wife."

"Marry you? But I thought the two of you loathed each other. I thought ..." Suspiciously, she studied each of them, her mother standing as though caught with her hand in the cookie jar, her—gulp—future stepfather smiling nervously. She noticed suddenly the way her mother's hair was mussed and how Sir Neville's cravat was twisted and crushed. A crimson blush stole across her cheeks.

"I ... I wish you very happy," said Phoebe, backing toward the door. "Excuse me," she whispered and fled.

"Phoebe! Wait!" called Annabelle. "What about your necklace?"

Neville unfolded his long legs and stood, an infuriating grin on his face.

"This is all wrong," whispered Annabelle.

"Don't worry, my dear. She'll get used to the idea," said Neville.

"But I ..." Annabelle paused, her resolution faltering.

"We should be getting downstairs," said Neville, coming to stand behind her at the mirror.

Annabelle shivered when his hands touched her shoulders, slipping down and encircling her waist. He placed a tender kiss on her neck, searching her face in the mirror, enjoying the image of domesticity.

"You must fix your cravat," said Annabelle, trying to sound brisk instead of breathless. "The chamber across the hall is empty."

"Very well," he said, his smile teasing her. "I will go and leave you to complete your toilette. 'Twould be best to go down separately. We wouldn't want any gossip to soil my fiancée's reputation."

He released her and strolled to the door, opening it slightly to be certain the corridor was empty. Turning back to Annabelle, he stated, "From now on, every waltz is mine, my love."

The door closed behind him. Annabelle sat down and began to pin up her hair. It was almost like starting over, and she contemplated ringing for Mary, but she wanted no company.

"You've done it now," she told her image.

Downstairs again, Annabelle circulated through the guests. Since this was not her house, and it was not for her daughter's engagement, there was no need for her to join her host and hostess in the receiving line. Instead, Margaret had assigned Annabelle to make certain the guests were kept happy with champagne and that the wallflowers danced at least every other dance. In this, she had enlisted Phoebe's help, telling her daughter to attach several of the less fortunate girls to her side. The young men in her coterie, all gentlemen, would perforce ask each of the young ladies for at least one dance.

Annabelle nodded to Phoebe across the room and smiled. Phoebe lifted her chin and turned away.

"She will need time to grow accustomed to the idea," said Neville, appearing at her elbow.

"Sir Neville, we must talk," said Annabelle.

"The next set is to be a waltz; we can talk then," he said, giving her elbow a proprietorial squeeze before moving away to speak to friends.

Annabelle signaled a nearby footman to fetch her something to drink. He returned, quite naturally, with a glass of champagne. Annabelle downed it with daring speed and requested another. Dutch courage, she thought grimly.

The strains of the first waltz brought Neville to her side once again. Annabelle pasted a smile on her lips.

After several moments, Neville commented, "You're very quiet, my dear."

"Am I? I suppose it is the surprise," she said, forcing a smile to her lips.

This is more difficult than I anticipated, she thought. I didn't expect to enjoy his touch, and certainly not his kisses.

The maxim about cutting off one's nose to spite one's face swam before her mind, but she banished it ruthlessly. Physical attraction was not a sufficient foundation for a marriage, she reminded herself.

"I suppose we should decide on a date for the wedding," said Neville, his steps leading her into a twirl. "I should like it to be as soon as possible," he continued with a slow, lecherous smile.

"But Phoebe . . ." she hedged.

"This is the second week of May. Would the first of June suit you?"

"I . . . I'm not sure. Let me think . . ."

"Very well, but I should tell you I have obtained a special license," he said. Leaning close to her ear, he added, "Then if you decide you simply can't wait, we can be married at a moment's notice."

Annabelle pulled away and forced herself to smile brightly. The tears in her heart threatened to spill, but she forced herself to remember the pain and humiliation he had caused her.

Was all of this just a game for him, too? she wondered. Perhaps he would withdraw his offer on the morrow, relishing the feeling of power over her. He must think himself princely indeed to be able to win her back with a mere word or two.

But she would show him the meaning of disappointment, she thought, her heart protesting against such cruelty to the man she loved. Used to love, her mind rebutted harshly.

The music ended, and Neville reluctantly relinquished her to her next partner.

"So, have the two of you made up?" asked Sinbad.

Neville turned to study his friend, resplendent in a white satin waistcoat and a cobalt blue coat. "You cut quite a figure tonight," he said, grinning.

"None of that," said Sinbad. "Charlotte thinks I am very dashing. Mind you, it's a bit more risqué than my usual, but a fellow only celebrates his engagement once."

"How right you are," said Neville, his smile growing. "I suppose, being your best man, that it would be suitable to tell you, in the strictest confidence, that I would like for you to return the favor—quite soon."

"What?" exclaimed Sinbad, attracting interested listeners. "You're going to be married?"

"Keep your voice down, you clodpole," hissed Neville.

"Oh, oh, right. Terribly sorry," said his friend. Sinbad whispered hoarsely, "To Lady Fairfax?"

"Who else," said Neville, rocking on his heels. "But tell no one until it is official, understood?"

"Perfectly."

"Not even Charlotte," warned Neville.

Sinbad appeared affronted and drew his dignity around him like a cloak. "I do not tell my affianced bride everything."

Across the room, Phoebe's bright red curls were bent to dark as she and Charlotte put their heads together.

"He was in her room?" gasped Charlotte.

"Yes, and you'll never guess what they told me." Phoebe paused for dramatics before continuing, "They are to be married!"

"Married! Sir Neville and . . ." exclaimed Charlotte before Phoebe could clap her hand over her friend's rounded mouth.

"*Shh!* I'm not certain they want it spread about yet."

Charlotte nodded solemnly. Studying Phoebe, she asked, "How do you feel about this?"

"I don't know precisely. While I want Mother to be happy, I'm not at all certain Sir Neville is the right man for her. Where will they live?"

"More to the point," said Charlotte sagely, "how will it be having Sir Neville as your steppapa? He is so . . ."

"Interfering?" supplied Phoebe.

"I was going to say shrewd, but either description applies. He could certainly dampen your spirits."

Phoebe appeared to be considering the matter. Smiling, she said, "To be quite truthful, Charlotte, the idea is rather daunting. Perhaps I should find a way to thrust a spoke in their wheels."

Annabelle passed the next hour in a daze. Each time she spied Neville, he was gazing at her soulfully—almost, she told herself cynically, as if he really loved her. Really, she must put an end to this masquerade as quickly as possible.

When the second waltz of the evening began, Annabelle took the coward's way out and disappeared. When Neville found her, he swept her onto the dance floor without preamble and demanded an explanation. Her haughty reply that she was helping repair someone's gown did not appease him, and he held her stiffly for the remainder of the dance. This second waltz caused speculation among the other guests, but Annabelle and Neville were too self-absorbed to notice the sly looks they were receiving.

When Neville held her hand a little too long after the music ended, Annabelle blushed, gave a quick curtsey, and hurried away, leaving the gossips more food for thought. With a frown, Neville left the ballroom to join the card players in the large salon.

The third waltz was the supper dance, and Neville sought out Annabelle eagerly.

"I'm afraid I can't, Sir Neville. I'm needed in the kitchens. Some crisis . . ." As luck would have it, the butler appeared by her side at that very moment and whispered something in her ear. With a quick apology, Annabelle hurried away.

Sir Neville, left to his own devices, for he had no intention of taking to the floor with anyone else that evening, watched the other couples turn and dip as the music swelled and fell.

After a few moments, he noticed that something was causing the dancers to turn their eyes in his direction each time they passed. Looking behind him, he saw only other guests deep in conversations. Frowning, he glared back. The whispered words and titters continued until he sought refuge in the dining room, where the servants were putting the final touches on the sumptuous display.

Annabelle hurried through the door that led down to the kitchens, smiled his way absentmindedly, and disappeared again. Glowering at the elaborate ice sculpture in the center of the groaning table, Neville loaded a plate and retreated to a chair at the table nearest the kitchen door.

The music ended, and the guests began to stroll into the dining hall, exclaiming appropriately at the turtle dove ice sculpture and the white, wrought-iron birdcages with live doves located at each end of the table. The birds, cooing contentedly when it had been only a few servants and Sir Neville present, took exception to the sudden crowd and became agitated. The soothing sounds were gone, and the resulting fracas had guests holding their ears. Lady Sweet sat down in a swoon while Annabelle reappeared and summoned several strong footmen to pick up the huge cages and follow her out of the room.

Having been bribed throughout the evening by Lord Sweet's excellent champagne, everyone took the disturbance in good part, their jovial remarks soon teasing Lady Sweet back into high spirits.

Neville found himself cornered by a number of chaperons who instinctively searched out the least desireable table near the kitchen door. Their mousy demeanors and timid voices apologizing profusely, they offered to set him free to enjoy the delights of other ladies. Only a cad would have accepted their offer and deserted them, so Neville, his whole being on the alert for Annabelle, kept them entertained by recounting mild scandals, waiting for his love to appear.

Annabelle came up the back stairs and circled to the ballroom. She peeked around the corner, amused to spy Neville with his mature harem.

To accommodate the many guests, tables spilled out of the dining room and into the ballroom. Urged by some acquaintances to join them, Annabelle sat down in time to hear Lord Sweet's formal announcement of Charlotte and Sinbad's betrothal. Everyone clapped and toasts were made all around.

Lady Goforth leaned over to Annabelle and whispered hoarsely, "I suppose we have to wait awhile before we get to hear your announcement.'' She winked knowingly.

"I don't know what you mean, my lady,'' said Annabelle.

Lady Goforth took another sip of champagne and nodded slowly. "I understand,'' she said, cocking her head toward the doorway to the dining room. "It's Miss Sweet's night.''

"I really don't know what you mean, Lady Goforth.'' Annabelle's hauteur was ineffective with her inebriated listener.

"You know, Sir Neville and you . . .''

Annabelle's cheeks responded with a telling blush, and the other occupants of her table leaned closer.

"Some interesting news?'' asked Mr. Kemp, one of London's most notorious gossips.

"No, I assure you . . . There is no news, nothing,'' said Annabelle, her agitation growing.

"But I overheard—''

"Nothing,'' said Annabelle, throwing a significant look at Lady Goforth, who ignored it completely.

"You know, I also overheard an interesting tidbit, but I discounted it. However, my lady, if there is something to it, you can easily set things straight. Why, I am the soul of discretion, I assure you,'' said Kemp, almost salivating over the delicious gossip.

"There is no tidbit, no truth,'' said Annabelle, rising and glaring at each occupant of the table before adding, "If you'll excuse me? I am needed in the dining room.''

A flurry of conversation propelled her on her way.

Annabelle's heart was beating irratically; things were getting out of hand. She had told no one about their false betrothal, but Neville had been very busy indeed. Annabelle stopped in her tracks.

Fool! she thought. You never warned Phoebe to keep the news confidential! If Phoebe had . . .

Annabelle shuddered. This was not at all what she wanted to have happen. Teaching Neville a well-earned lesson had been her original object, but making him the butt of a scandal was unthinkable!

Her own embarrassment had been a private thing. No one had known she had given her heart to a man who cared nothing for it or her. Her misery had been solitary. But if word of this so-called betrothal had gotten out, Neville's embarrassment would be public, and for such a proud man, it would be unbearable. Although she had reason to despise him, could she bear to be the cause of his suffering? She must tell him, and quickly, that she could not marry him. And she should warn Phoebe . . . If only it was not too late!

But still Annabelle hesitated. She told herself not to be swayed by her emotions, but still she agonized over ending this mock betrothal. If only . . .

But no! she told herself, her mind once more controlling her thoughts. He didn't love her; he never had. He wanted her; of that, she had no doubt. And she could even admit that she felt the same keen desire for him, but it would never do. She could never be happy, married to a man who didn't love her.

She would carry through with her plan, she resolved. Before the night was over, the next time there was an opportunity for private conversation, she would tell him, in no uncertain terms, that she could never marry him. She would take him aside . . .

Annabelle watched as Neville entered the ballroom, on each arm a giggling, elderly woman. How kind and charming he is, came the unbidden thought.

Then panic gripped her. Oh, given a chance, he could be very charming and disarming! She simply couldn't allow him the opportunity to be alone with her when she broke off their betrothal!

Then tranquility returned to her breast. It would have to be during the final waltz, she decided. Until then, she would simply avoid him as much as possible. After all, she comforted herself, he couldn't very well make a scene, or worse yet, make love to her, in the midst of so many people!

Annabelle managed to remain elusive until the fourth and final waltz of the evening, but there was no escaping, and she steeled herself to resist the fire of his touch and concentrate on the task before her.

Feeling neglected and disgruntled, Neville scowled at her as he guided her onto the floor, ignoring the surprised onlookers and the wave of whispering. He caught phrases like, "Hasn't danced with anyone else," "as good as caught," and "announcement by tomorrow."

He couldn't hide his displeasure; it showed in every part of him: in his eyes, his mouth, and the way he held her so much more formally. He was not pleased with Annabelle or with himself; he felt awkward and foolish. Neville was no longer the man of cool cynicism he had once been.

Recognizing this made him more annoyed than ever, and he snapped, "Where did you disappear during supper?"

"Disappear? Why, I was tending to the needs of the guests. I believe I mentioned that I had offered to do that so Margaret could enjoy herself this evening without worrying about any silly little details," said Annabelle, her eyes frosty.

"Yes, yes, but did you have to miss the entire meal?"

"I didn't. I looked in from the ballroom; you were being entertained admirably, so I took a chair with Lady Goforth."

"Entertained?" he said sourly. "I was waiting for you."

"I had no idea," said Annabelle, opening wide those green eyes which had bewitched him so. "I had no idea you were so moody."

"That really depends on you, my dear."

"On me? Do you mean any time I express an opinion that differs from yours, or if I do something to displease you, you intend to punish me with churlish behavior?" said Annabelle, warming up to the theme.

Neville looked puzzled. "Not at all," he said quickly. "I'm sorry. I suppose I did sound churlish."

"You most certainly did," said Annabelle in a tiny voice he had to strain to hear. "I never realized you were such a bully."

Alarmed and annoyed, he snapped, "Bully? I have never been accused of being a bully! What nonsense is this, Annabelle? What is the matter with you?"

"Matter?" she continued, persisting in the most pitiful tones. "Why, nothing is the matter with *me;* you are frightening me, that is all."

"Frightening you? What nonsense!" said Neville, perplexed. Never in a million years would he have fallen in love with such a mousy thing as Annabelle was acting. *And I haven't!* he thought. *She is up to something, and I intend to force her to explain!*

"It is not nonsense," whispered Annabelle.

"Yes it is, and if you persist in this nonsensical manner, I shall be forced to stop in the midst of all these dancers and kiss you senseless!" he declared with a leer.

Annabelle missed her step and almost fell, stopping completely when Neville caught her. Motionless in the center of the ballroom, the other couples continued to dance past. All eyes were on the stationary couple.

Her voice low but clear, Annabelle looked him in the

eye and announced, "Then I am afraid, sir, that I must inform you that we should not suit after all. I must break off our betrothal." She turned on her heel, leaving an astounded Sir Neville in her wake.

Chapter Fourteen

Sir Neville awoke in a cold sweat. Panting, he lay quite still, willing the remembrance to have been only a dream. But it hadn't been a dream, and in the darkness, he cursed Lady Annabelle Fairfax, using army vocabulary he thought he had long since forgotten.

And then he cursed himself for a fool, no better than a callow youth who fancies himself in love with an opera singer.

Rising, he stumbled to the basin and poured some tepid water, splashing his face several times. He heard the clock that stood at the end of the hall chiming the hour—five o'clock. He had slept less than two hours.

Not bothering to ring for his valet, Neville pulled on some old clothes and worn riding boots. He made his way down the back steps that led to the kitchen and was soon outside, breathing deeply; the house had threatened to suffocate him. He walked silently to the stable and saddled his horse, moving stealthily to avoid waking his groom, who slept in the tack room.

The stall door creaked when he closed it, and he paused, waiting to continue.

"Major?" said the sleepy voice with the heavy Spanish accent. "Do you want me to harness the horses?"

"Go back to sleep, Antonio," he barked. "I'm just going for a ride."

"*Sí*, major," said the boy, rubbing his dark, sleepy eyes with one hand and scratching his ribcage with the other. He watched in silence as Neville mounted, and then hurried to open the back gate, standing at attention as his master rode past.

Neville turned the horse toward the park, the hooves clattering noisily in the silence of the early dawn as they cantered past the sleeping houses. When he reached the entrance to Green Park, Neville pulled back on the reins, staring into the gloom. He looked up; the stars were fading as the sun began to peek over the horizon. It was going to be a beautiful day, clean and fresh after yesterday's rain.

With a quiet curse, Neville turned away from the park and kicked the gelding's sides, urging him forward, faster and faster, past Hyde Park, until they were well away from the neat rows of houses and shops and people. His horse winded, he slowed it to a walk. Turning off the main road, he finally stopped when he reached a small stream.

He dismounted and sat down on a large rock; leaning back on his elbows, he stared at the sky. His horse drank noisily and then moved closer, giving his master a wet nudge.

"Sorry, old boy. I didn't think to bring any carrots or sugar this time," said Neville, stroking the velvet nose. The gelding blew air out his nose and began to crop the green grass.

Neville closed his eyes and slept.

The sun was uncomfortably warm by the time Neville awoke. He got on his feet and stretched before whistling for his horse. There was an answering whinny, and the gelding trotted back to him.

"Good boy," said Neville, stroking the glossy neck. "At least I can always count on you; you're a good soldier." The big horse whickered and butted him gently in the chest. "We went through hell together in Spain; I suppose we can make it through this, too," he said.

It was afternoon before Neville returned to the stables; he ordered an extra ration of oats "for his friend." Once upstairs, he relaxed in a steaming tub of water, a glass of Madeira in one hand and a full decanter by his side.

Maltby entered the room, sending his valet away with a turn of his head.

"Pour yourself a glass, Maltby. I feel like celebrating."

"And what are you celebrating, sir?" asked the former batman, pouring a glass and moving the decanter to the dressing table.

The gesture was not lost on Neville, and he grinned before responding to his friend's question, "Freedom, Maltby. Sweet, complete freedom."

"I've heard a little here and there about your freedom, sir. I'm sorry."

Neville pierced him with his silver stare and said firmly, "Sorry? It was the best thing that could have happened. I must have been mad ..." But Neville's dark thoughts threatened to overwhelm his bravado, and he ruthlessly shoved them out of his mind. "I will be fine, Maltby. I'm not going to drink myself senseless as you fear. I am going to dress, go down and eat an elephant or two, and then go to my club. After a few hands, I shall probably attend the theater. No need for you to worry about me; no need at all.''

"As you say, sir. I'm very glad to hear it," said the old man, his face reflecting his relief.

Neville was as good as his word, and if his card playing was more ruthless, no one seemed to notice. His coldly calculating moves brought him the lion's share of the winnings, but this could hardly be considered remarkable. All in all, Neville managed to fool everyone else that he cared not a whit what the gossip mill was saying.

As for his own feelings, he kept them close and controlled.

Exhaustion had afforded Annabelle a better night's sleep than she had had in weeks. But she stretched lazily, opening her eyes reluctantly to the day which was already so advanced. She heard a noise and looked up; Mary entered carrying a tray with a steaming pot of coffee and a plate with some toast.

"Good morning, my lady," she said cheerily, placing the tray across Annabelle's knees before going to open the curtains. "A beautiful day today. I'm that glad to see the sun."

"It only rained for a day, Mary," grumbled Annabelle, sipping her coffee. "A little rain is necessary for the flowers, you know."

"I know, my lady. I'm a farmer's daughter, make no mistake. But rain at home and rain here are two different things."

"I suppose so—somehow it seems gloomier here. Perhaps it is all the gray in the buildings; in the rain, a body can hardly tell where they end and the sky begins."

"Exactly," said the maid. "Will you be wanting a morning gown, my lady, or a carriage dress?"

"A carriage dress, I think, since the hour is so advanced. Charlotte and Phoebe both have fittings at one o'clock. I'll barely have time to dress as it is."

"And what would you like to eat? There's a bit of kidney pie left," said the maid.

"No, I'm just not hungry, Mary," said Annabelle. Then, acknowledging the look of concern on her maid's face, she relented, "Just bring me some fruit and cheese, Mary."

"I'll see what I can find in the kitchen, my lady. I'll be back in a trice," said the maid.

"Thank you, Mary. You're a gem."

The maid blushed prettily and hurried away.

Annabelle took another sip of coffee before setting the tray aside and climbing out of bed. She looked into the garden below and managed a smile. It was truly amazing how a bright sun could affect one's outlook. Perhaps she would be all right.

There were only a few short weeks before she could return home. Until then, she would do as she had always planned, chaperon the girls and see the wonderful sights of London. Her afternoon today was full, but on the morrow, she would again visit the Royal Academy, this time with only her sketch pad and her maid Mary as companions.

Annabelle knew she would no longer be troubled by Neville; his fury the night before had been palpable, but she had seen no sign of pain. So she had done the right thing; he had only wanted to possess her; it was not love which had made him propose. The thought made it possible for her to shut out the pain of losing him.

Mary returned carrying another tray. "Here's some cheese and bread, my lady. There's also a sliced apple."

Returning to bed, Annabelle sat with her legs crossed,

partaking heartily of the cheese and apple slices. To her surprise, she found she was truly hungry.

Mary brought out a gray carriage dress, and Annabelle said, "Oh, not that one, Mary. Let's have something more cheery today. How about the coral sarcenet?"

"Very good, my lady. You look ever so pretty in that," said the abigail.

"Thank you, Mary. And thank you for this wonderful breakfast. Now I shall be able to keep up with those two girls today," she said, her cheerfulness becoming less forced.

"You are looking very cheerful today, Mother," said Phoebe, eying her mother with open curiosity when they were settled in the carriage for the ride to Madam Lemieux's shop.

"Thank you, my dear. I feel exceptionally fine today," said Annabelle before turning to look out the window.

Phoebe and Charlotte frowned at each other; Annabelle could see them out of the corner of her eye, and she smiled. Let them wonder, she thought.

Madam Lemieux had a full shop, but her best seamstress was waiting for Charlotte and Phoebe in the largest chamber. Charlotte's wedding gown was hanging on a dressmaker's dummy, its beauty absolutely breathtaking. Charlotte's eyes filled with tears, and Phoebe handed her a handkerchief impatiently.

"Silly goose," she said fondly.

"I'm sorry, but it is so beautiful. I can't believe I will be wearing it," said Charlotte.

"First, Miss Sweet, we must make certain it fits," said the seamstress, an elderly woman whose squint and stern mouth would have given fright were it not for the nervous smiles she flashed every few seconds. "It will look beautiful on you, but we want it to fit perfectly. Only then will you do it justice.''

Phoebe and Charlotte exchanged grins over the woman's bent head, but they contained their laughter. Annabelle excused herself and left to wander in the front room where all the latest materials and fashion plates were on display.

Examining a bolt of finest India silk in a cornflower blue, she heard her name. Turning around, she surprised the gossips, a Lady Thurmond and her boon companion Mrs. Paxton.

"Oh, my dear Lady Fairfax, what a surprise to find you here today," said Lady Thurmond. "You are acquainted with my friend Mrs. Paxton?"

"Yes, we have met on several occasions. Good afternoon."

"Good afternoon," said Mrs. Paxton.

Annabelle returned to her browsing, frowning as she heard their whispered conversation. Mrs. Paxton was urging Lady Thurmond to "draw her out on the subject."

With a marshall light in her eyes, Annabelle turned to them, holding the silk in her hands. "Is this not the most exquisite color you have ever seen? I generally favor greens and reds, but this blue is simply divine."

"Yes, it is beautiful," said Lady Thurmond, "But that garnet gown you wore last night was so fetching. Speaking of the ball, Lady Sweet really outdid herself. The refreshments, the music, the entertainment—all extraordinary."

Mrs. Paxton took up the sword and continued coyly, "I understand there was more than one betrothal last night."

"Whatever do you mean?" asked Annabelle.

"Well, I . . . That is, they say you and Sir Neville . . . ?"

Annabelle said frostily, "I'm afraid you are mistaken."

"But the times you danced together . . . And I heard from Mr. Kemp . . ." said Lady Thurmond, her disappointment showing plainly in her droopy eyes.

Mrs. Paxton, however, all but rubbed her hands and said mournfully, "How sad for you that the arrangement didn't work out."

Annabelle pulled back. "Sad? I assure you, Sir Neville Colston and I had no arrangement."

Looking over their shoulders, her two listeners moved in closer. Mrs. Paxton asked with sugary sweetness, "Was there some lovers' quarrel between you and Sir Neville?"

Annabelle's brow shot upward, and she looked down her nose at Mrs. Paxton. "I can see you are determined to believe in idle gossip. Good day."

"Idle gossip cannot compare with three waltzes, Lady Fairfax," said Mrs. Paxton with an evil smile.

"Mother, will you join us for a moment?" called Phoebe.

"Excuse me," said Annabelle, hurrying away. At the doorway, she turned and watched as Lady Thurmond and Mrs. Paxton dropped the fashion plates they had been examining and hurried out the door. The story would make the rounds by nightfall. She had underestimated the Ton's adoration of gossip. She had been naive to think there wouldn't be gossip, not after she had danced with Neville thrice and then left him standing on the dance floor. She must think of some way to extricate them from this terrible bumblebroth.

After their fittings at Madam Lemieux's, the girls wanted to visit the lending library, and Annabelle agreed, not wanting to return home any sooner than necessary for their afternoon callers.

When they entered Hookman's, Annabelle sent the

girls off to find the latest romance novels, saying she wanted to find a particular book on art.

In reality, she had spied the notorious gossip Mr. Kemp and wanted the chance to converse with the fidgety little man. Kemp had left the ball early before that last dance, but judging from the manner in which he bore down on her, he had already heard of the scandalous goings-on. If she could convince him that the rumors were all a hum, he would soon spread the word.

"Good afternoon, my dear Lady Fairfax. We are happily met. I see you have brought your beautiful daughter and her charming friend, the bride-to-be of Mr. Sinclair." Annabelle nodded, and Mr. Kemp continued. "I, too, have been dragooned to come. My niece and sister are here somewhere."

"I would like to meet them," Annabelle said quickly.

"And so you shall," he breathed, "but first, you and I must have a comfortable coze. Do come and sit with me for a few moments."

When they were seated, he whispered confidentially, "I understand congratulations are in order."

"Congratulations?"

"Yes, yes, you needn't play coy with me. I am as discreet as a cadaver, I promise you."

"I wouldn't dream of casting aspersions, Mr. Kemp, but I'm afraid I don't know why you should be congratulating me."

He wagged a short, stubby finger under her nose, and said, "I have heard all about your betrothal to Sir Neville."

"But you are mistaken, Mr. Kemp," said Annabelle, looking distressed.

"Now, now, I know all about that last waltz when you left him dangling in the middle of the ballroom, but come now. Lovers often quarrel, and I'm certain you and Sir Neville will soon patch things up."

"Please, Mr. Kemp, I must beg your assistance in this matter. There is nothing between me and Sir Neville. You must believe me and help me."

"Help you, my lady? I would be delighted. Only tell me how I may be of service," said the little man, licking his lips.

"It is most distressing, Mr. Kemp, that no one will believe me when I say I am not betrothed to Sir Neville, that there is absolutely no truth to the rumors going around."

"But, my lady," he said, sitting back and gazing at her with his incredulous, beady eyes. "Surely you know dancing with the same man three times is tantamount to an announcement."

Annabelle shook her head and said, "But that is for young girls surely."

"That is for anyone, especially when neither you nor Sir Neville danced with other partners," he said, shaking his head. "So you see, no one will believe—"

"Oh, but they must! I won't have people saying I am going to wed where I am not!" exclaimed Annabelle, her voice rising. "Please, Mr. Kemp, you must help me convince everyone!"

He patted her gloved hand, and Annabelle had the urge to wipe it clean, but she didn't want to offend this powerful little man.

"It will be difficult, but I will think of something, my lady," he said, his eyes lighting with anticipation. "Now, if you'll excuse me?"

"Certainly, sir, certainly," said Annabelle, feeling more at ease as she watched him toddle out the door, forgetting all about his niece and sister.

* * *

Sir Neville frowned. Something was definitely wrong—something more than the anger and hurt he still suffered from Annabelle's actions the previous night.

He had decided to attend every function for which he had received invitations in an effort to squelch any rumors circulating about the night before. Therefore, he found himself at an extremely dull musicale, wondering why he was being avoided by almost all the females present.

"Good evening, Mrs. Paxton, Miss Paxton," he said, smiling in a friendly manner at this lady and her shy daughter.

Mrs. Paxton grabbed her offspring's arm and hustled her away without acknowledging his greeting.

"What the deuce?" he muttered.

Lady Beresford began shooing her guests into the ballroom, which she had set up as a music chamber. "Hurry, everyone, the diva is about to begin. Oh, Sir Neville, good evening. I . . . The entertainment is about to begin," she said nervously.

Neville looked down, wondering idly if he had forgotten his pantaloons. No, he was decently clad, everything covered as Society decreed.

The butler admitted Sinbad Sinclair, and he greeted Neville in a friendly manner.

"Finally," said Neville, "someone who doesn't shrink from me as if I were the devil himself."

Sinbad looked at the ceiling and shuffled his feet.

"Not exactly the devil. It depends on which tale they have heard," he explained reluctantly.

"Which tale?" asked Neville, a slow anger starting to simmer.

Sinbad took his friend's arm, saying, "Come along. We'll go into the dining room. It should be empty, and I feel the need for sustenance, or a large glass of port at the very least."

"You make me more and more apprehensive," said Neville.

"It is like this," began Sinbad when he had taken a large gulp of the fiery liquid. "Someone is putting it about that the reason Lady Fairfax broke off your secret betrothal is because you are a fortune hunter."

"A fortune hunter!" he exploded. "Where the devil did such a ridiculous tale get started? And who would believe it? It's not as if I don't pay my gaming debts."

"I know that, and so do your other particular friends, but Kemp was at the club comparing you to that loose screw who tried to kidnap that widow last year, you remember, the Irish one, Lady Fitz-something."

"I'll call him out," growled Neville.

"Can't do that," said Sinbad. "Kemp is such a puny, weak thing, and well liked despite his penchant for gossip; people would only say that the other story must be true then."

"What other story?" asked Neville warily.

"Oh, well, this one is a little more difficult to trace. I don't know the original source. I heard it at Jackson's boxing salon late this afternoon."

"Pray continue," said Neville ominously.

"Yes, yes, well, it's a rather delicate topic," hedged Sinbad, shifting uncomfortably on his chair. Other guests, tiring of the music, began to drift into the room. Sinbad sensed his chance slipping away and said baldly, "It seems she refused you because you have certain unusual habits . . . with the ladies. Ludicrous, of course, but rumors usually are."

"Damn," whispered Neville.

"Most people won't believe it, of course, but there you have it, Nev. It's hard to fight rumors," said Sinbad.

"It can't have been her," murmured Neville, looking beyond his friend and catching a glimpse of auburn hair. Annabelle's face appeared, her eyes drawn to his immediately. Her cheeks flamed.

"It must have been!" he growled. Without another word, he rose and started for the door. Annabelle lifted her chin in defiance, but he passed her without so much as another glance. She bent her head, tears starting to her eyes. So much for her newly acquired peace of mind!

Chapter Fifteen

Margaret, appalled by the rumors, sought out Annabelle and regaled her with the lurid tales. Annabelle denied all knowledge of the rumors, but in her heart, she knew her conversation with Kemp had been the fuel for the flames.

"I don't see how he can show his face! And he is to be the best man at Charlotte's wedding! What are we to do?"

"Surely you don't believe any of these lies!" exclaimed Annabelle.

"It doesn't matter if I do or not; we simply can't have him standing up with our Charlotte!" said Margaret, fanning herself rapidly. "I must ask Lord Sweet to speak to Sir Neville immediately."

"It really isn't your choice, Margaret. Mr. Sinclair is the one to choose his best man. You have no say in the matter."

"I shall speak to him immediately!" exclaimed Margaret, turning to hunt down her future son-in-law.

Annabelle wished for the night to end.

"Mother, I have just heard the most extraordinary tale," said Phoebe.

"I know. Lady Margaret just told me about it."

"But Mother, I thought you and Sir Neville were betrothed."

"*Shh!*" hissed Annabelle, taking Phoebe's arm and propelling her to a more private place. "Sir Neville and I did speak about the subject, but we decided almost immediately we shouldn't suit. It was a mutual decision. You didn't tell anyone about the betrothal, did you?"

Phoebe blushed and confessed, "I told Charlotte, Mother. I thought Sir Neville was telling the truth!"

"No, I mean yes, but it is more complicated than that."

"Then the rumors, are they true?"

"Of course not! Sir Neville is a fine man; he is simply not the sort of man I could wed. He is far too sophisticated and frivolous for me."

"I see," said Phoebe doubtfully.

"Good, now we'll speak no more about it. And when you see Charlotte and Lady Margaret, please tell them I would like to go home."

Annabelle faced the following day through guilt-colored spectacles; the thought produced a small laugh which could have passed for a sob. Dressed in a pale lilac morning gown, she entered the breakfast parlor in time for luncheon and addressed all her attention to her plate.

Lord Sweet hid behind his newspaper, but Margaret was still abed. Phoebe and Charlotte chattered about inconsequential subjects, steering clear of the betrothal ball and the previous night's musicale, which was clearly on everyone's mind. Annabelle gave them a weak, but appreciative smile as she slipped from the room and wandered outside.

Margaret had warned her after Charlotte's ball that her name would be the talk of the clubs, but she hadn't listened. She had said she didn't care, that she was only getting back at Sir Neville after being humiliated by him. Reflecting now on Margaret's words of censure, Annabelle could only be sorry she had not heeded her friend's advice and kept silent on the matter. She wished devoutly that she could escape.

After being so humiliated at the theater, when she had all but begged Neville to bed her, she had "run away," supported by her indignation and hurt pride. Now, she couldn't run away—not with Charlotte's wedding the first week of June.

The first of June! That is the date Neville suggested for our wedding, came the unbidden memory.

You're a fool, she told herself. *What does it matter if the only feelings he has are physical desires? You love everything about him, from the top of his head to . . . Surely,* she chastised herself, *that would have been enough!*

Now, of course, she had much more to be ashamed of after the lies . . . Not that she had told Kemp to spread such outrageous rumors! But she had asked him to do something, anything! Annabelle tried to justify her actions by remembering Neville's treachery, but it brought very little consolation. It wasn't his fault he didn't love her. She had tried to play by his rules, the rules of the Ton, but she was not equiped for meaningless flirtation, and she had been burned.

Annabelle took a deep breath, the fragrance of the roses filling her senses. Slowly, she unbent her fingers, which had been gripping, white-knuckled, the stone bench where she sat.

"Mother?"

"Yes, Phoebe?" she said, forcing a smile for her daughter. "Join me," she added, moving to one side of the bench.

"Mother, I know that you are no longer betrothed to Sir Neville. I don't pretend to understand what that was all about." Annabelle nodded solemnly, and Phoebe continued, "All I want to know is, are you happy?"

"Happy?" echoed Annabelle, her voice hollow, devoid of emotion. "I think, Phoebe, that I will be happy again when we go home. This Season has been very long."

Phoebe chuckled. "Long to you, but much too short for me."

"I'm glad you have enjoyed yourself. You have changed a great deal; a little town bronze has done you good, I daresay."

"I think so," said Phoebe. "And Mama, Charlotte has asked me to come back during the Little Season."

Annabelle expressed surprise, saying, "Surely you don't mean to stay with the newlyweds? The house Lord Sweet is giving them as a wedding present isn't very large."

"Oh, no, Mother. I shan't stay with them! But Lady Margaret has invited me to stay here again. You are welcome, too, of course."

"No, Phoebe, I don't think I will be able to return in the fall. It's a very busy time, what with the harvest and all. But you should come back, although I think things are a little slower during the Little Season."

"Ah, but that was before I came to London," she said, her mischievous grin bringing a smile to her mother's eyes. Then she added gravely, "You won't be too lonely without me, will you?"

Annabelle patted her hand and shook her head. "I shall be too busy to miss you too much. Have you forgotten what it is like when the harvest comes in? But you will come back for the Harvest Festival, won't you?"

"I wouldn't miss it," said Phoebe, hugging her mother impetuously.

Sir Neville was in a foul mood; his temper was so short, his servants started hiding from him. He took no interest in his appearance, driving his exacting valet to distraction. He drank far too much, worrying his old friend Maltby. And he refused to attend Sinbad Sinclair's nuptials, angering his friend, who was forced to cope with his intended bursting into paroxysms of sobs.

He was not embarrassed to go into Society. The rumors Annabelle had started would soon blow over, and the people he cared about wouldn't believe them anyway. But he was outraged by her betrayal. If she hadn't wanted to marry him, then why had she ever agreed—even briefly? It was as if she were bent on revenge. But revenge for what? he wondered.

There was no real reason; he admitted that they had had their misunderstandings, but nothing to make her despise him, he didn't think—not, he admitted, that he was thinking very clearly.

So he was less than pleased when Phoebe Fairfax, never one to shrink from her duty, paid an afternoon call on him, scandalizing his entire staff.

Lifting his head from his desk where he was napping in a port-induced slumber, Neville grumbled, "Send the chit away."

"But sir," began Peters.

"Never mind, Peters," said Phoebe, slipping inside the study and staring derisively at Sir Neville. "I will take care of this. Bring some coffee, if you please, very strong."

"Yes, miss," said the butler.

"And how long since he has eaten?" she asked, studying him in a detached manner and speaking as if he were a child or pet.

"Last night, miss."

"Then bring some sandwiches as well. Nothing too spicy or greasy."

"Very good, miss."

When the door had closed on the butler, Neville looked up and said, "Go away, Phoebe. I don't want you here."

"No doubt, but you have no choice. I daresay I could beat you in any form of combat at the moment, and I know absolutely nothing about fisticuffs."

He gave her a lopsided smile. "Saucy wench," he muttered, pushing away from the desk and rising. He waited a moment to be certain he could stand before making his way to the sofa—slowly, so he wouldn't stumble and fall in front of Phoebe.

When he was comfortable, he pointed to a chair, saying crossly, "You may as well sit down since you're here."

"Thank you," she replied, arranging her skirts carefully before looking back at him. Peters entered with a silver tea tray, setting it in front of Phoebe. "Thank you, Peters. This looks wonderful."

Phoebe popped a sugary biscuit in her mouth before pouring the coffee. "Hmm, these are delicious, very buttery. Would you care for one?"

"Just give me the coffee," he said.

"You really should have something to eat also. Do

you realize it is three o'clock in the afternoon? You should be starving!"

"Well, I'm not!"

"Very well, there's no need to be unpleasant." Phoebe took a sandwich and bit into it with enthusiasm. Next, she sampled the Sally Lunn cakes and pronounced them fit for a king—or a queen, she added with a laugh. Neville watched in silence. Brushing the crumbs from her fingers, Phoebe eyed him with displeasure. "If you're going to pout, I might as well leave."

"Then why don't you do so? And I am not pouting," he said. Leaning forward, he picked up two sandwiches and quickly ate them. "Now are you satisfied?"

"Not yet," she said sweetly. "I will only be satisfied when you agree to stand up with Mr. Sinclair as you originally intended."

"Sorry, but I can't do that."

"It's really no use to refuse as I intend to plague you every day until you agree again."

"I'll have the door barred," said Neville, grinning despite himself.

"I daresay your staff would let me in; they seem to think you need looking after."

She has me and she knows it, thought Neville, his gray eyes narrowing. But Phoebe only ate another biscuit, ignoring his menacing glare.

"Oh, very well. I can't afford to have you visit every day. The housekeeper would demand more money for food and ruin the household accounts," he said, his grin returning as she hugged his neck impetuously.

"Oh, thank you, Sir Neville, thank you! I must hurry home now and tell Charlotte. She will be delighted! Good day, sir. A very good day to you indeed!" She paused at the door and turned, her smooth brow furrowed.

"Was there something else you wished to plague me about?" asked Neville.

"I . . . You should know, Sir Neville, that Mother had nothing to do with those terrible rumors, nothing at all."

"You'll forgive me if I doubt you on that point. I happen to know she was seen speaking to Kemp the day after the engagement ball, and he is the one who started both rumors."

"Perhaps, but Mother would never stoop so low."

"Goodbye, Phoebe," said Neville, relaxing against the cushions to steady the throbbing in his head. After a moment, he gathered his strength and bellowed, "Maltby! Peters! Get in here!"

His two senior retainers appeared instantly; Neville guessed quite correctly they had been listening at the door during Phoebe's visit.

"What are you gaping at?" he growled. "Have Higgins draw me a bath. Send for the barber. Oh, and send some flowers to Miss Sweet for me, begging her pardon. Well, what are you waiting for?"

Smiling happily, they hurried to do his bidding.

"I am certain I shall faint," said Charlotte, peeking into the crowded church.

"You will be fine," said Phoebe. "You look beautiful; every man present will be sorry he is not the fortunate groom."

"You are beautiful," said Charlotte's father, smiling at his eldest daughter indulgently, his chest swelled with pride.

"There's Sinbad," whispered Charlotte, her eyes softening, her fidgeting ending suddenly. "I'm ready," she announced calmly.

Charlotte's sisters, from the youngest to the twins, served as bridesmaids. They were dressed in virginal white with pink rosebuds in their hair. Phoebe wore a pale pink gown with white rosebuds adorning her flame-colored locks.

All eyes were on the bride as she ascended to the altar. When Charlotte passed, Annabelle took Margaret's hand and squeezed it gently. They both held handkerchiefs at the ready.

Turning to face the couple at the altar, Annabelle felt a jolt of surprise. She had steeled herself for this, seeing Neville at the ceremony, but her preparation had gone for naught. His dark good looks and height made him stand out from the other figures. He wore gray this morning, his waistcoat a dark burgundy, the epitome of quiet elegance. He was smiling slightly as he listened to the couple's vows.

Annabelle closed her eyes as tears started to fall. She dabbed at them, glad to be in a situation where tears were common and would attract little attention.

She had been a fool! She should have married him when he asked. What did she care if he didn't truly love her? But she did care. And so the vicious cycle begins again, she thought bitterly, her tears falling in earnest.

The wedding breakfast at the Sweets' town house was another sumptuous affair. It was also very merry with countless toasts being proposed—some rather tasteless, which caused Margaret to send her other daughters back to the nursery.

There was an orchestra and soon the dancing began, Charlotte and Lord Sweet leading out the first waltz, taking one turn before her father surrendered her to Sinbad. Others soon joined them, the ballroom quickly filling with graceful figures. Annabelle smiled as Phoebe and Lord West passed her, then returned to her melancholy state.

A few short weeks ago, it had been she and Neville in each other's arms in this very ballroom, she thought. Sensing his eyes on her, Annabelle looked across the room. Neville lifted his champagne glass to her, his expression thoughtful, perhaps even melancholic.

If only I could believe, thought Annabelle, her eyes filling with tears. She slipped away from the celebration, telling herself it wasn't right to exude such regret on this joyous occasion.

Neville sealed the missive and handed it to Antonio, not releasing it until he had secured the tiger's promise to give it to Lady Fairfax personally.

"I promise, major, sir," said the young man with a wink.

Neville did not spoil the groom's romantic illusions by revealing the true reason for his letter. Instead, he flipped him a coin and urged him to hurry.

In truth, Neville was uncertain what would come of his request to see Annabelle. Would she agree to see him to "iron out their differences"? What would she expect from him?

As Annabelle read Neville's note, her color drained from her face, causing Antonio to exclaim in alarm.

"I'm fine," she said, her voice suddenly hoarse with emotion. She took a deep breath and reached for pen and paper. "You'll take this note directly back to Sir Neville?"

"Of course, milady," he promised.

When he had gone, Annabelle smiled. Now, she told

herself, now you will have the chance to apologize to him. After that, you can rest easy.

A wicked voice teased, This time don't waste precious seconds with words—kisses are much more effective. She shook her head, refusing to listen. There was no reason to think Sir Neville wanted anything from her; he had stated that he merely wanted to clear the air and suggested a quiet picnic in the countryside.

The wicked voice asked her which gown she should wear, suggesting the green one that suited her auburn hair so well and had a deep décolletage to show off her generous bosom.

Annabelle ignored the voice and picked up a book.

An hour later, Phoebe entered and turned it right-side-up for her.

The day for their picnic was warm and humid; clouds gathered in the distance. Annabelle waited in the drawing room, her dark green gown covered by a long, sensible spencer. She had twisted her hair up and pinned it on top of her head, allowing a few escaped tendrils to soften the severity of the style.

He is late. It is a quarter past ten; perhaps he isn't coming, she thought, not knowing whether to feel relief, disappointment, or annoyance. The latter won out when she finally heard the door open at half past the hour.

Neville bowed before her, the action stiff and formal. Annabelle frowned, but she rose and took his proffered arm. When he had handed her into his curricle and climbed in after her, he smiled and apologized prettily, but his eyes remained wary.

They drove in silence through the crowded streets until they reached the countryside.

"I thought we would find a spot near Richmond, somewhere along the Thames, if that suits you."

"That sounds very nice," said Annabelle, telling herself to relax.

Neville guided the grays off the main road and drove through a series of small tracks, little more than footpaths. Trees threatened to block their passage, then suddenly thinned. Neville stopped the team on the edge of a secluded clearing. They could not see the river, but could hear it flowing lazily nearby.

Neville jumped to the ground and turned to catch her around the waist and swing her down easily. His hands held her for a moment before he grinned and released her, moving to the back of the curricle where a basket was lashed securely.

Annabelle strolled toward the sound of the water while Neville spread a blanket and set out the food his cook had lovingly prepared.

Wandering back to the clearing, Annabelle said, "You should walk down to the river; it is lovely. There is a green pasture on the other side with sheep and a cow grazing."

"Very pastoral," said Neville, patting the blanket by his side. "Join me."

Annabelle sat down and allowed him to fill her plate. She laughed when he handed it to her.

"Do you really expect me to eat all of this?" she asked.

"I don't, but my cook most certainly would. However, I promise not to tell if you don't," he confided with a grin.

Their eyes met, and the amusement faded, replaced by some unfathomable emotion.

Turning away, Neville said briskly, "Let's see what Peters packed for our wine. Ah, a light burgundy. Will you join me?"

"Yes, I believe I would like a glass," said Annabelle, thinking she needed a very large glass to steady her nerves. Studying him through her lashes, she wondered if he was affected as strongly as she. Probably not; after all, he wasn't in love with her as she was with him.

"To understanding," said Neville, raising his glass for a toast.

"Understanding," she responded, drinking deeply.

Neville drained his glass and poured another. "To friendship," he said.

"Friendship."

Neville drank deeply and raised his glass once more. "To love," he said, winking at her.

Annabelle watched as he finished the second glass. He had no intention of clearing the air, she thought angrily. She started to rise, but he caught her wrist.

"Don't go, Annabelle," he said, pulling her down.

"I think we should both go, Sir Neville," she whispered, wishing his burning touch did not have the power to engulf her in flames.

"And I," he said, ignoring her suggestion and pulling her closer, "think we should both stay."

When his lips touched hers, Annabelle lost all desire to leave. Neville moved the glasses and plates while his kisses enslaved her. Somehow, she found herself lying on her back, his body pressing hers into the soft grass.

The fire within her was contagious; Neville's tongue darted in and out of her mouth, his hips matching each thrust. Annabelle felt the cool air bathe her breasts as he released them, the low-cut gown pushing them upward for his lips to pleasure. All rational thought vanished as she wrapped her legs around his thighs.

His hand worked the fabric of her gown up to her waist, and she began to tug at his breeches. She groaned in frustration when she failed and thrust her hand between their bodies to feel his desire.

Moaning, kissing, stirring, and matching his rhythmical thrusts, Annabelle gasped, her breath suspended as wave upon wave of complete pleasure rippled through her body, finding its way, eventually, to her intellect.

Neville rose up on his palms so he could watch her as the insanity of passion slowly released her. Annabelle's eyes were dazed, and she blinked several times, trying to reconnect her thought processes with her sight.

Neville laughed at her owl-like appearance and rolled off her. He rose and turned his back to adjust his too-tight breeches.

"I always knew you were a passionate wench," he said, chuckling quietly.

Annabelle scrambled to her feet, his laughter taunting her, shaming her. What had she done? All he wanted was to humiliate her. So that was what all this was about, this picnic, the wine, the . . .

Blindly, she stumbled toward the curricle. Raindrops began to fall, and Neville reached down to retrieve his coat and shrug into it. The seat of the curricle creaked as she climbed in; she glanced back at him as he lunged for the reins. Annabelle threw off the brake, and the horses shot forward.

"Annabelle! What's the matter? Annabelle!" he shouted, but she was already whipping up the team of grays, sending them plunging through the trees.

Chapter Sixteen

Shaken and horrified by her own actions, Annabelle was glad when the team entered the heavy woods and was forced to slow their pace. She had driven carriages pulled by two horses before, but not the bits of prime blood like Sir Neville's pair of grays. The horses, walking now, came to a complete halt. Annabelle picked up the ribbons and slapped their rumps cautiously, but they refused to move.

"Easy, easy," said a low, calm voice.

Annabelle whirled around, cringing as Neville picked his way through the brush and climbed up beside her.

Without a word, he took the reins from her unresisting hands and backed the horses and equipage out of the dead end. Silence predominated all the way to the main road. Once they were tooling swiftly toward London, he glanced at her sideways.

"We've made a rare muddle of everything, haven't we?"

Annabelle nodded, but she remained silent and kept her eyes fixed firmly on the road.

Neville sighed. "I shan't be troubling you again, my lady," he said, his voice tinged with a note of regret.

The buildings began to close in on them, and Annabelle patted her hair into place, wishing she had not left so precipitously, forgetting her bonnet.

Neville pulled up at her door and didn't bother to descend. He waited until she was out of sight before he pulled away, sending his weary team home at a plodding walk.

Annabelle found it impossible to concentrate as the next few days sped by; the day set for their return to the country was imminent. She and Phoebe were to depart the same day the Sweets left for her sister's country home to spend the remainder of June and the hot days of July and August.

There was only one major entertainment left before their departure—Lady Grosbeck's masqued ball. Phoebe had talked of nothing else but her costume for the entire week since Charlotte's wedding. Charlotte, too, had wanted to attend, but the promise of a wedding trip to France had made her forgo the ball. Phoebe refused to reveal any details of her costume, promising her mother it would be very appropriate.

Annabelle, still aching for what might have been, decided to simply trust her daughter's judgment. As for Annabelle, she had settled on a purple domino with a matching mask. All she could think about was the day after the masquerade when they could return home.

Lady Grosbeck lived on the edge of London; for her ball, she had commissioned the erection of five different tents, each one reminiscent of a different era. Knowing many guests would dress in medieval style, one tent had gaily colored flags flying above it and "walls" of exquisite tapestries. Suits of armor were arranged here and there, and the servants all wore armor breastplates and shining helmets. The second tent had no tables or chairs; huge pillows were scattered here and there and the servants wore turbans and costumes of desert sheiks. The third was from the time of Elizabeth I; the servants wore ruffs around their necks, tights, and doublets. The fourth tent was full of Grecian urns and fit for a Roman orgy. The fifth was a bit macabre; the tent was enclosed and the interior was lighted only by red lanterns. The servants wore bed sheets with holes cut out for their eyes.

Phoebe had discovered the plans by flattering Lady Grosbeck's shy son. When she came down the stairs, she wore a bed sheet with holes cut for the eyes.

"Why were you so secretive about your costume, Phoebe? There will be any number of ghosts," said Lady Sweet.

"Oh, really?" she asked, her worried tones sounding forced to Annabelle. But Margaret announced it was time to leave, and the trio, a little dull because of Charlotte's absence, set out for the masqued gala.

Annabelle listened as Margaret cautioned both Phoebe and her about the relaxed manners one sometimes encountered at masquerades. Annabelle listened in dismay; Phoebe, with glee.

Phoebe wasted no time in losing herself among the other revelers. Dressed in her bed sheet, she had little fear of being molested. No one could be certain she was a female, despite her short stature. But Phoebe didn't remain a ghost for long.

As soon as she had watched her mother and Lady Margaret drift into the medieval tent, she made straight for the Elizabethan tent. Scanning the guests, Phoebe quickly spotted her quarry. In a black domino and mask, Sir Neville Colston, true to Maltby's prediction, was dancing attendance on Lady Rand-Smythe, whose costume proclaimed her to be a well-endowed Elizabeth I. Maltby had also reluctantly revealed to Phoebe that Sir Neville had spent much time trying to get back into that lady's good graces since his picnic with Lady Fairfax.

Phoebe didn't care what he had been doing. She only knew that her mother was miserable and wouldn't be happy until she became Sir Neville's wife—even if her mother didn't realize it herself yet.

Phoebe stepped behind the tent and removed her bed sheet. She tied on a purple mask that matched her domino and slipped casually back into the tent. The lighting inside was dim, and as long as she stayed on the far side, she felt confident her ruse would work.

Grabbing the arm of the nearest waiter, she handed him a note. "Take this to the gentleman over there with that Queen Elizabeth," she said.

Phoebe watched while Sir Neville read the note. She cocked her head to one side and smiled at him—seductively, she hoped. Sir Neville glanced down and read the note again. When he looked up, she was gone.

Behind the medieval tent, Phoebe met Lord West and Goodie. Being the taller, Goodie had been selected for the mission. Wearing a black domino and mask and clutching another note Phoebe had written earlier, he entered the tent where Annabelle sat talking with Margaret and several other matrons.

He stuck his head back outside and whispered, "She's dressed just like you, Phoebe."

"Of course she is, you looby," said Lord West.

"Oh, right," said Goodie. He instructed a waiter to give Lady Fairfax the note and waited, waving—suavely, he hoped—when she looked up. Then he ducked out and hurriedly turned his domino inside-out, changing it to a deep red.

The three of them hastened away.

Annabelle clutched the note tightly, smiling at her interested observers. "Just a note from Phoebe. Seems she has torn her sheet." At their startled gazes, she added hastily, "She came as a ghost. If you'll excuse me."

Annabelle paused outside the tent and held up the note to the candlelight, reading it once again. There was something familiar about the handwriting. Had she ever seen Neville's writing? she wondered. She sighed and walked decisively beyond the tents to the gazebo, which was beside a moonlit ornamental pond. It was certainly romantic, and his note had been so very apologetic. He said he loved her. She doubted it, of course, but she felt she should at least hear what he had to say.

There he was, waiting inside the small wooden structure. Annabelle stepped inside and hesitated.

"Good evening, my lady," said Neville, stepping forward but holding himself aloof. When she didn't speak, he asked, "Well, what was it you 'particularly' wanted to say to me?"

"I wanted to say something to you?" asked Annabelle.

"That's what your note said."

"My note? No, that's what your note said."

"I don't know what you are talking about," said Neville, removing his mask so that his frown was much fiercer.

Annabelle held out the note; not to be outdone, Neville produced the note he had received, and they scanned them quickly.

"Phoebe!" they both exclaimed.

"I am so very sorry, Sir Neville. I assure you I had nothing to do with this," said Annabelle, backing away.

The moonlight touched his face with shadows; his expression looked amused and sad, and his tone sounded wistful as he said quietly, "I never thought you did." He started forward and extended his arm, saying formally, "Allow me to escort you back to the masquerade, Lady Fairfax."

"Thank you, Sir Neville," said Annabelle, her heart breaking as she backed away. "I can manage on my own."

Annabelle, who had hardly slept in the days preceding the disastrous masqued ball, was up early the next morning, directing Mary and the footmen on the disposition of her cases.

"Where is Phoebe?" she asked when the hour of ten had sounded, and the girl still had not appeared. "She knew I wanted to get away early."

"I'll go check on her, my lady," said Mary.

"Annabelle, we are ready to leave," said Margaret, peering into the cluttered room. "Oh, you are not finished yet."

"Don't worry about us, Margaret. Phoebe can never leave anywhere on time, as you know. Why don't you go on. You needn't wait on us."

Margaret hesitated. "I hate to leave you like this."

"Don't worry, it is not as bad as it looks. We shall be on our way by noon at the latest, and our journey is not as long as yours."

"True, and you know how Lord Sweet hates delays. Very well, my dear, we shall go ahead." She moved forward to hug Annabelle; fortunately, it was a brief hug or Annabelle felt she might have suffocated in her large friend's massive bosom. "I will miss you. I promise I will pay you a visit when we come back to town in September."

"Thank you so much for inviting us, for all you have done for me and Phoebe," said Annabelle, ready tears springing to her eyes. "Have a good journey. Goodbye."

"Goodbye, my dear," said Margaret, dabbing at her eyes as she left the room.

Annabelle heaved a sigh and returned to the task at hand. Mary hurried in, wringing her hands and frowning.

"What is it?" asked Annabelle sharply, thinking that Phoebe was probably up to another of her queer starts.

"Oh, my lady, it's Miss Phoebe, she's sick. I felt her forehead, and it was on fire!"

Annabelle didn't waste words but hurried directly to Phoebe's room. It was dark inside, but she could see the figure in the bed try to rise up on her elbows before collapsing back against the pillows.

"Phoebe," she said, trying not to show her alarm. "What is wrong, dearest?"

"I don't know, Mother. I just woke up feeling so weak."

Annabelle placed her cool hand on her daughter's forehead; it was hot, but moist. Then she took her wrist and felt for the pulse; it was shallow and rapid.

"I want to go home, Mother," whined Phoebe.

"We will, sweeting, we will. Just not today. Mary, send one of the footmen for the physician."

"No!" cried Phoebe, lifting her head weakly. Relaxing again, she said, "I don't want to see a physician. I'll be fine in a day or two."

"Nonsense. Mary," said Annabelle.

"Yes, my lady. I'll send Robert immediately. The others all have plans to leave on holiday this afternoon."

Annabelle sat on the side of the bed, wringing out a cool cloth and placing it on Phoebe's brow.

"You just rest, love. I'll be right here," said Annabelle. For a fleeting moment, she thought she saw Phoebe smile, but a closer look revealed nothing.

When the physician arrived, Annabelle stepped into the hall to confer with him before he entered the room. Mary remained with Phoebe.

He was dressed formally, his coat of an excellent cut. His reputation was the very best, but he was known for his stern bedside manner. Speaking to the beautiful Lady Fairfax, however, his demeanor softened. He went so far as to smile at her.

"It came on so suddenly, Dr. Knightsbridge. I'm very worried," said Annabelle.

"I daresay you have nothing to worry about, my lady. These young people have little fevers that come and go, but I'm glad you called me. I'll have a look and set your mind at rest. Although, I see you are closing up the house and preparing to leave for the summer."

"Yes, Lord and Lady Sweet left this morning. My daughter and I were supposed to be away by now, but she is too ill to travel."

"Don't you worry, my lady. We'll soon set her to rights. You'll be away before you know it. Now, if I could see the young lady?"

"Of course," said Annabelle, her hand on the latch. They heard a loud clunk, and she opened the door, asking anxiously, "What was that?"

"Nothing, my lady," said Mary. "I just dropped a . . . something."

Annabelle was too focused on her daughter to notice the maid's nervous explanation.

"Phoebe, here is Dr. Knightsbridge to see you."

"What? Oh, the physician," she said, opening her eyes and peering at him.

"Now, Miss Fairfax, when did you begin to feel ill?'

"When I woke this morning," she said, her voice little more a whisper. "Mama, I am so thirsty."

Annabelle poured some water immediately, her brow creased with worry. Phoebe hadn't called her "Mama" since she was a little girl.

"Drink this," she said, helping Phoebe to sit.

Dr. Knightsbridge pulled back the covers to listen to her chest. "What is this?" he asked, pulling two hot water bags out and holding them up.

"If it please your lordship," said Mary. "She did have such bad chills before you came; I only thought to warm her up."

"Ah, of course. You did the right thing, young woman. We must keep her warm," he added, replacing the water bottles.

A few moments later, he paused outside the door, shaking his head. "I'm afraid we will simply have to wait until other symptoms appear, my lady."

"Other symptoms?"

"Yes, a sore throat, congestion of the lungs, perhaps. Or she may wake up in the morning fit as a fiddle. I have left some laudanum if she should become restless. I don't expect it, mind," he added, patting Annabelle's shoulder in a fatherly manner. "Send for me if she should worsen in the night."

"Thank you, Dr. Knightsbridge. I'll just see you out."

"No need, my lady. I can find my way. And remember, you are not to worry; she appears to be a strong, healthy girl. She'll come about, you'll see."

"Thank you again," said Annabelle. She opened the door and motioned to Mary to join her in the hall.

"Yes, my lady?" said the maid anxiously "He did say Miss Phoebe would get better, didn't he?"

"Yes, yes. You mustn't worry so. He told me the same thing. He thinks it just a passing fever, but I fear we will be remaining here for a day or two longer. How many servants are still here?"

"There is the butler, my lady, and perhaps Robert, although he did mention going to visit his mother."

"Well, I suppose we can make do. I'll go down to the kitchens to see what is left in the larder. I may have to go to the market. You'll stay with Phoebe?"

"Of course, my lady. I'll stay right by her side."

"Thank you, Mary. I don't know what I would do without you," said Annabelle.

"Oh, my lady, don't say that," cried Mary, covering her face with her apron.

"There, there, Mary, you are just upset about Phoebe. Now, compose yourself and go back to Phoebe. I'll be back as quickly as I can."

For Annabelle, it was one of the longest days of her life. The gloom in Phoebe's room filled her heart, and she found it impossible to occupy the time even with her needlework.

When evening fell, Annabelle thought Phoebe's fever was lower, and she allowed Mary to sit with Phoebe while she went down to the kitchens and prepared some soup from potatoes the butler had discovered in the larder. There was some stale bread left, and she filled the tray with enough provisions for two.

The butler carried the tray, and they made their way back up the stairs. Annabelle touched Phoebe's forehead; it was much hotter than before.

"Mary, I don't like this," she said quietly while Phoebe groaned and shifted in the bed.

"She was quiet until you came back," said the maid.

Annabelle shook her head sadly. "You go down and eat; I'll see if I can get her to take a little soup."

Phoebe refused to eat, falling into a fitful sleep while Annabelle forced herself to swallow the thin soup. I will need my strength for tonight, she thought dismally. Guiltily, she recalled the last four days, wondering if Phoebe had been sickening, but she had been too wrapped in her own misery to notice.

Annabelle shook off the guilt. That was one thing it would certainly do no good to dwell on. She opened the curtains and a light breeze cooled her face.

When Mary returned, she insisted on staying with Phoebe and commanded her mistress to go to her room and sleep. Annabelle, worn-out with worry, complied.

Annabelle found it difficult to sleep; she woke every few minutes and listened, thinking she had heard Phoebe calling for her. Once, she even threw on a wrapper and hurried to Phoebe's side, only to discover her daughter seemingly peaceful, if still hot and sleepless.

Returning to her bed, Annabelle felt more hopeful, and was soon sound asleep. Her dreams were sweet this time, not troubled. She was lying on the ground, staring at the sky while clouds drifted slowly past. He was there, of course; her happy dreams always contained him, perhaps always would, she thought, sighing contentedly in her sleep.

"Mother, Mother."

Annabelle's eyes flew open, and she hopped out of bed, astounded to see Phoebe leaning on the door frame of her room.

"Phoebe! Are you all right?" she demanded, rushing to her daughter's side.

Phoebe collapsed against her.

"Mary! Mary! Come quickly!"

If Annabelle had been alert to the maid's appearance, she would have noticed Mary was crying already. But concern for her daughter superseded all other things, and she was only conscious of the need to get Phoebe back to her own bed.

When she and Mary had safely tucked Phoebe in, Annabelle said worriedly, "I think you should fetch the physician, Mary."

"No, no, Mama, I want Sir Neville. I must see Sir Neville," wailed Phoebe.

"Sir Neville?" exclaimed Annabelle, backing away from the bedside, frowning heavily. "What is she talking about?"

Mary shrugged and said, "I don't know, my lady. Do you think I should fetch Sir Neville?"

"Certainly not!" snapped Annabelle. "He is not a physician!" Phoebe moaned Sir Neville's name again, and Annabelle rushed to her side, chaffing her daughter's wrists and cooing reassurances, but Phoebe kept moaning for her nemesis.

Tossing and turning, Phoebe continued for several more minutes before Annabelle came to a decision.

"Very well, Mary, take Ames and fetch the physician and . . . Sir Neville."

"Immediately, my lady," said the maid, sailing from the room.

Phoebe continued as before for another five minutes and then grew quiet. So quiet, Annabelle leaned anxiously forward and listened to her daughter's chest. Slow and steady. She felt Phoebe's forehead, but it was surprisingly moist and only warm, not hot.

Twenty minutes passed before she heard noises below. She rose from the bedside and moved to the door to consult with the physician. Sir Neville appeared at the end of the corridor, his long stride gobbling up the distance in seconds, leaving her no time for thought.

"How is she?" he demanded.

All of Annabelle's anger disappeared, and she fell into his arms, tears cascading down her cheeks while she sobbed uncontrollably.

Neville blanched and whispered, "Is she dead?"

Annabelle only shook her head against his chest, and he held her more tightly, stroking her hair and comforting her as he would a child.

When she lifted her face, he wiped her tears and gave her his handkerchief.

"Now, shall we go in and see how she is?"

"Yes, yes, we should check on her," said Annabelle.

When he took her hand, it seemed the most natural thing, and Annabelle didn't protest. They opened the door to blackness.

"What is this?" asked Annabelle, hesitating as she became accustomed to the darkness. The lamp in the hall threw enough light into the room to see the figure wrapped up in the bedclothes. "The candle must have blown out," said Annabelle.

"With the curtains drawn?" said Neville.

He led her into the room and threw the curtains wide. The moonlight filtering through the closed window showed plainly the frown on his face. Annabelle lighted the candles and gazed at the bed. With two steps, Neville joined her beside the bed, studying the lumpy covers. Annabelle gasped as he threw them back to reveal several pillows and a dozen hot water bottles. Then he heard the key turn in the lock.

"What the devil is this about?" he roared, turning on Annabelle.

"How should I know?" she retorted. "Phoebe! Where are you?"

Phoebe's laughter rang clearly through the empty house. "I am here," she called; her giggles precluded further comment.

"What is going on, Annabelle?" demanded Neville, his gray eyes turning to silver with anger.

"I don't know," snapped Annabelle, her own anger matching his. She strode to the door and tried the lock. It wouldn't budge. "Phoebe, open this door at once!"

"No, I don't think I shall, Mother."

"Phoebe, unlock this door," said Neville, his voice dangerously even.

"I'm afraid I must humbly decline, sir," she said, giving him her best flirting giggle.

"Phoebe, this is not funny. And you should be in bed," added Annabelle.

"She isn't ill," said Neville. "The chit's too mean to be ill."

Phoebe responded with laughter again. "You are so droll, Sir Neville. And very much in the right of the matter. I am not ill, nor have I been."

"Phoebe!" exclaimed Annabelle, her shocked expression causing Neville to grin down at her.

"I'm sorry, Mother, but I simply couldn't allow you to return home without Sir Neville. You have been miserable for weeks without him; I couldn't allow you to be miserable for a lifetime."

Neville watched with interest as Annabelle's face turned bright red, but she did not deny Phoebe's observations. He smiled, and she ducked her head.

"And you, Sir Neville. I have been in contact with Mr. Maltby; he and I have become quite good friends. He reports that you are in much the same case, except you have tried to drown your sorrows in the bottle. Not a healthy pastime, I'm sure you'll agree.''

It was Neville's turn to fidget uncomfortably while Annabelle raised her eyes, her mouth twitching with amusement.

"So, I decided to stage this little charade to give you time together to work things out between you. You may as well begin talking; I don't intend to unlock this door until morning," she announced smugly.

"Phoebe, this is ridiculous," said Annabelle, but her eyes were on Neville's warm gaze.

"Tomorrow morning," reiterated Phoebe.

"I suppose the dressing room door is also locked?" asked Neville.

"Of course," said Phoebe. "Now, I'm going to go sleep in your bed, Mother. By morning, I expect to hear wedding bells."

They listened as her footsteps faded away.

Looking at the floor, studying the ceiling, they waited by the door for a moment.

"I suppose she was serious," said Neville.

"I'll lock her in her room for a month," vowed Annabelle.

Neville laughed, saying, "Now that would be a fitting punishment." He reached up and smoothed Annabelle's untidy hair. She moved away from him, looking around the room in confusion.

Neville came up behind her and asked, "What is it?"

She turned to him, smiling ruefully, her eyes twinkling. "What is missing from this room?"

He surveyed the contents and grinned. "Chairs. There's not a single chair to be had. She is serious, isn't she?" he added, looking at the bed.

Annabelle felt suddenly shy next to him. She wandered to the window and leaned against it. Neville moved to the bed, sitting on the edge, bouncing on it, testing its softness.

"Come here," he said quietly. When she didn't respond, he said gruffly, "I shan't lay a hand on you."

Tears threatened, but Annabelle lifted her chin, looked him in the eye, and said stoutly, "That's what I'm afraid of."

"Annabelle," he said, rising and opening his arms. She fell into them, and he rained kisses on her before saying softly, "I love you more than life itself."

"You do?"

"Of course I do." Neville restrained the impulse to add, "you silly wench."

"I wasn't sure," said Annabelle. "You never told me before."

"Yes, I did," he said, his impatience growing.

Annabelle pushed back and looked him in the eye. "You told me you wanted me, you told me I wanted you, but you never said you loved me."

Neville stared at her in disbelief. "But how could you not know? Did you not feel it?"

Annabelle smiled and gave him a quick kiss on the lips.

"But I do love you, my dearest Annabelle, and I want to marry you." She smiled mistily, and he chuckled, saying, "You're not going to turn into a watering pot on me, are you?"

Annabelle shook her head and whispered. "Not as long as you continue to love me."

"That will be forever, my love, forever and ever," he said, gathering her in his arms and pulling her onto the bed.

His mouth sought hers eagerly, their kisses serving only to fan the fires that engulfed them. Annabelle's hands mirrored Neville's, exploring and exorting new levels of passion. Annabelle shrugged out of the sensible wrapper, and Neville divested her of her gown, pausing to revel in her beauty before his lips began their movement lower, slowly, attentively. The stubble on his chin gently grazed each nipple, the rough touch soothed immediately by soft lips. His hands kneaded her flesh, caressing and teasing.

With a moan of pure ecstacy, Annabelle sat up, her hands pulling feverishly, ineffectively at his clothes. Neville slipped off the bed, his movements urgent and uneven as he removed his coat and shirt. Annabelle rose, adding her efforts to his, tugging at his breeches, her breath catching in her throat as he was freed from his final restraints.

They fell backward, Neville's weight pressing her deeper into the feather mattress. His kisses slowed; Annabelle growled a ragged "Please," and Neville responded, his body answering hers as he whispered, "My sweet love."

Epilogue

"Time to rise and shine," said Phoebe, unlocking the bedroom and throwing open the door.

She froze, wide-eyed and open-mouthed as she stared at the couple in the bed.

"Mother!"

"Yes?" said Annabelle, sitting up, the sheet covering her naked breasts.

Neville pushed himself up on his elbows, his bare chest causing Phoebe to gasp.

"What do you want, daughter?" he growled, leaning toward Annabelle and kissing her bare shoulder.

Phoebe whirled around, her back to them.

"Daughter? This was *not* what I meant when I told you to talk things over, Sir Neville. I feel I must demand to know your intentions toward my mother!" Silence greeted this outburst, and Phoebe took a quick peek over her shoulder to find her mother and Sir Neville embracing, nuzzling each other's neck. *"Harumph!"*

"What? Oh, are you still here, Phoebe?" said Annabelle. "Please shut the door when you leave."

"Mother! How could you?"

"Isn't this what you wanted, my dear? For me to be happy? I can assure you, Phoebe, I am deliriously happy," laughed Annabelle.

"Mother, I . . . Sir Neville . . ."

"You may call me Papa if you wish, daughter, because I intend to treat you as my own. I will provide for you, protect you, and give you direction, should you require it."

"Oh no," moaned Phoebe.

"Oh yes. You'll find out what it's like to have a father looking after you."

"Mother! Surely you're not going to allow him to order my life!" said Phoebe indignantly.

"I would rather not discuss that right now. You and your steppapa can settle matters later," said Annabelle, unable to keep the gurgle of laughter from escaping and giving away the game.

"I know what you're about! You're trying to get back at me for last night!"

"Us? Why would we do such a thing? We want to thank you for it, and we shall," said Neville, leering at Annabelle. "But not now, Phoebe. Now you are decidedly *de trop*. Go away."

"Mother."

"Hmm?" she murmured.

"So when are you going to marry my mother, Sir Neville?" demanded Phoebe.

"This afternoon, I think," he said. Turning to Annabelle, he added, "I do still have that special license, my love. There is no need to wait."

"It looks to me as if you haven't waited at all," grumbled Phoebe.

"Goodbye, Phoebe," said Sir Neville.

"Goodbye!" she said, flouncing out of the room, shutting the door on them.

"Now, where were we, my love?"

Annabelle snuggled under the blanket, her hand trailing down his chest. "I was just about there," she whispered.

"Then pray continue, my sweet," said Neville, lovingly kissing the top of her head.

BOOK YOUR PLACE ON OUR WEBSITE AND MAKE THE READING CONNECTION!

We've created a customized website just for our very special readers, where you can get the inside scoop on everything that's going on with Zebra, Pinnacle and Kensington books.

When you come online, you'll have the exciting opportunity to:

- View covers of upcoming books
- Read sample chapters
- Learn about our future publishing schedule (listed by publication month *and author*)
- Find out when your favorite authors will be visiting a city near you
- Search for and order backlist books from our online catalog
- Check out author bios and background information
- Send e-mail to your favorite authors
- Meet the Kensington staff online
- Join us in weekly chats with authors, readers and other guests
- Get writing guidelines
- AND MUCH MORE!

Visit our website at
http://www.zebrabooks.com

LOOK FOR THESE REGENCY ROMANCES

ROMANCE FROM HANNAH HOWELL

MY VALIANT KNIGHT   (0-8217-5186-7, $5.50)

ONLY FOR YOU   (0-8217-4993-5, $4.99)

UNCONQUERED   (0-8217-5417-3, $5.99)

WILD ROSES   (0-8217-5677-X, $5.99)

THE WELSH MABINOGI

It is seldom indeed that a series which starts with the *éclat* and acclaim occasioned by the first volume, THE ISLAND OF THE MIGHTY, continues to be as well received and as powerful as its start.

But the second of Miss Walton's books, THE CHILDREN OF LLYR, with its gaunt prose expressive of high tragedy, was just as strong as the first.

And this, the third volume, is again remarkable—as much for the gentle humanity of its principal figures as for the massive strength and awesome dignity they display when their magic powers are invoked.

In THE SONG OF RHIANNON, Manawyddan, brother to the mighty Bran the Blessed, and one of the seven survivors of the tragic expedition to Ireland, unites with his long beloved Rhiannon. But much stands in the way of their happiness. Dread of the seeds of evil planted by the overthrow of the Old Ways, fear for the youthful recklessness of Pryderi, and something darker yet—for Rhiannon is not of this world, and somewhere, somewhen, the Gray Man waits to take his vengeance and claim his own.

Adult Fantasy by
Evangeline Walton

**THE ISLAND OF THE MIGHTY
THE CHILDREN OF LLYR
THE SONG OF RHIANNON**

Published by Ballantine Books